M

U

STUFF
+THINGS

H

A

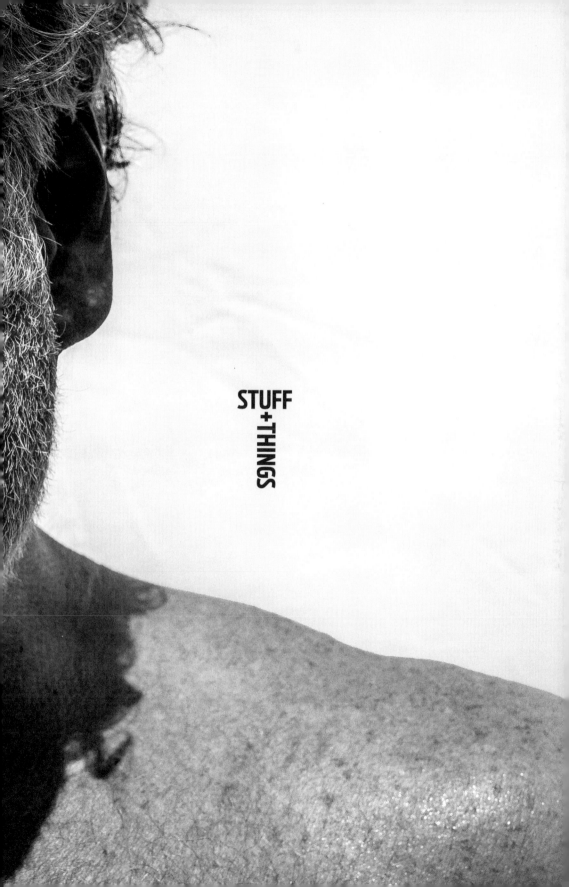

STUFF
+THINGS

CAMERON + COMPANY
Petaluma, California

M
U
H
A

STUFF
+THINGS

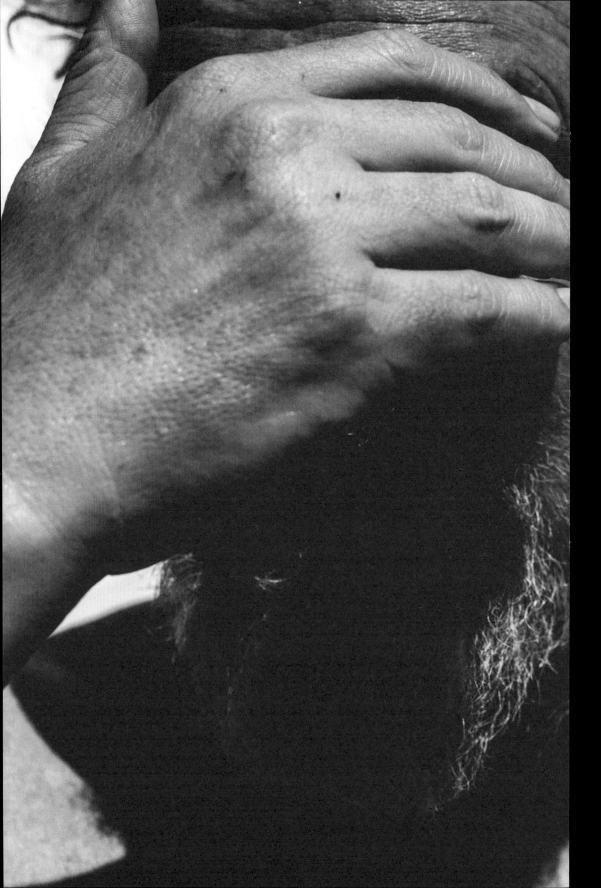

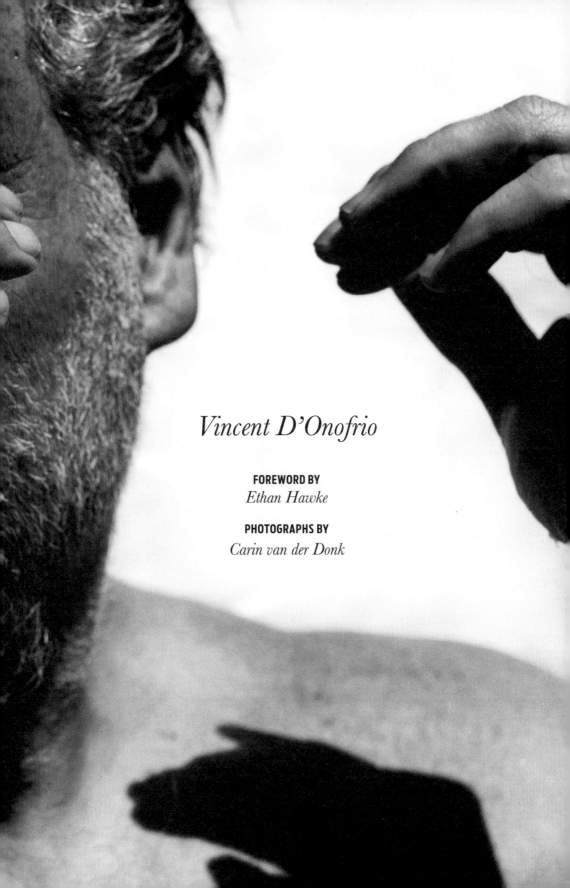

Vincent D'Onofrio

FOREWORD BY
Ethan Hawke

PHOTOGRAPHS BY
Carin van der Donk

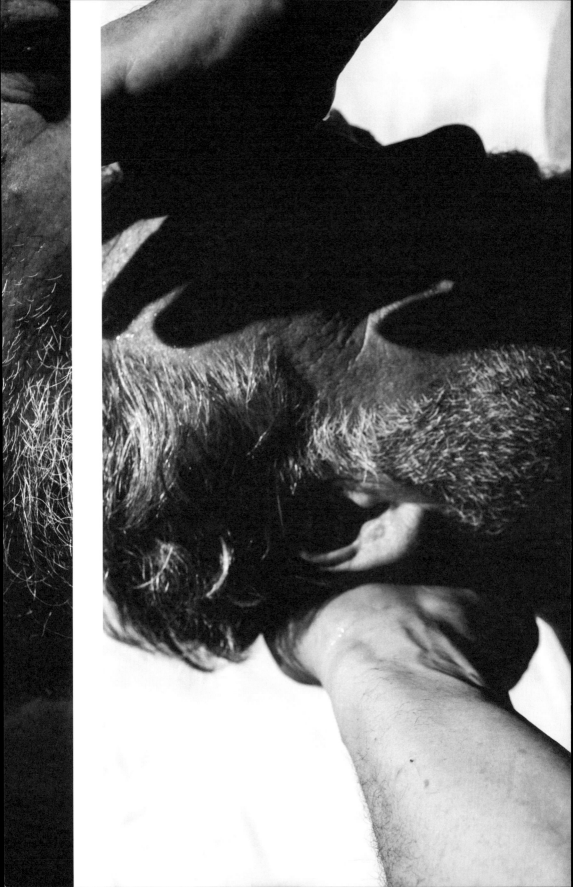

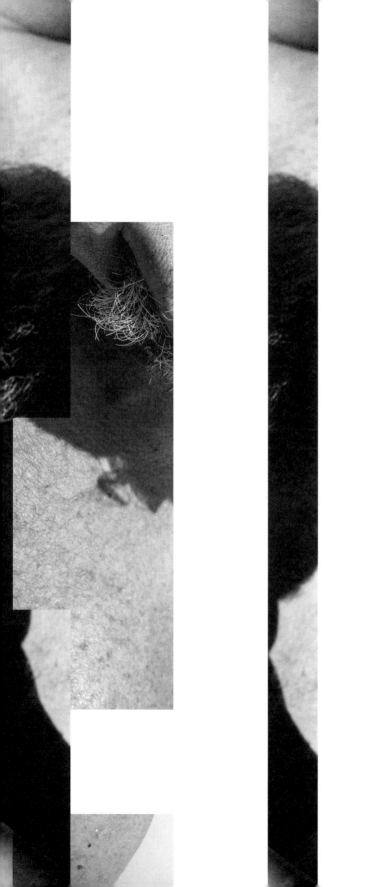

What if I had a secret and it mattered so much to you that your life would revolve around whether you ever found out what my secret is?

It's a secret.

BY *Ethan Hawke*

We were performing a play called *Clive*. It was an adaptation of Bertolt Brecht's incendiary first play, *Baal*. It is not for the faint of heart. The play has disdain for the audience. Lore has it that Patti Smith once said it's her all-time favorite. She may be the only one. Many audience members seemed actively angry with me for producing, directing, and starring in this show. The set was built out of beer cans and musical doors. Sounds strange and it was . . .

Early in rehearsals I remember telling the company that if critics or audiences liked this play, it meant we did it wrong. We all laughed confidently. But courage was hard to maintain as people argued in angry voices in front of the theater, sure there was no point to what we were doing. Even family members seemed slightly scared for us. We all want to be liked. We want to be understood. Young actors don't dream of walkouts. No one craves derision.

But there was a moment backstage, early in the run, when our collective mettle was being tested. Were we going to have the guts to deliver the nihilistic rage Brecht was asking for? I had called for a company meeting, hoping to boost a flagging morale . . . but my own confidence had waned and was so shaky I had little to offer. I was worried I had led all my friends down a dark hole from which no light could be offered. It was obvious to the cast I had lost my footing and was unsure how to lead. Vincent D'Onofrio spoke up and said, "I have something I'd like to read. I wrote a journal this morning."

We sat and listened. At first everyone was fidgeting and nervous. Is this for real? Is this supposed to be funny? Is this tragic? Is this the truth? By the end, we were howling like a pack of wolves at the moon. More journals followed. Something utterly original was flowing out of Vincent. We began gathering before every show, hoping for a new journal. Maybe it was Brecht's punk rock spirit that called to Vincent. Maybe it was just his own desire to heal and give confidence to his friends, but as this writing continued to pour out of him, one thing was clear: this shit needed to be published.

Things that have been told to me by animals
who don't speak or communicate.

16

MUTHA

THINGS THAT HAVE BEEN TOLD TO ME BY
ANIMALS WHO DON'T SPEAK OR COMMUNICATE.

1.

I'm a Mouse in a Red Dress

20

I'm a mouse in a red dress. I have a black nose
and I love cheese sooo much. I can balance
on a thimble with one foot. One foot. Imagine
that. I can run under a rug, sniff about, and
run out the other end. I'm a mouse in a red
dress. Imagine that.

I'm a cricket in a top hat. I'm soooo smart. Like
a spring, my legs sprang and I'm four feet in
the air. I land on a lawn chair, adjust my hat,
and I'm off. Another four feet and I land. I'm
on a garden hose and I'm a cricket in a top hat.
Sooo smart and I'm off again . . .

I'm a monkey in Miami Beach. I have a red
pillbox hat and a vest with tassels. I hate my
clothes but they are tied to me. I am in a palm
tree hiding in between a bunch of coconuts.
I will only come down to steal food. I've run
away from a stinky man with a beard and a
music box. I hate him; I hate the box. I'm a
monkey in Miami Beach.

I'm a crocodile with no friends. I'm still hungry.
I'm a crocodile with no friends.

I'm a tadpole. Jesus, I give up.

22

2.
I'm a Dog

I'm a dog and I love myself too much. I'm on a corner talking to my friends, and my owners are talking to their friends. Jeez, I feel a tingling sensation around my groin area. Should I have a sniff down there? I think I will. Fuck it, I think I'll lick my balls.

I'm out and about and wander into a store that allows pets. People can sometimes be such suckers for a cute face like mine. They have no idea what I'm thinking. Most likely I'm thinking about food. Or my groin is tingling like right now. I think I'll have a lick.

I wonder what the rest of the day will be like. I think I'll have a nap. I wish I had something to chew on. Like a baby bird carcass. Hey, there's a bunch of little children to play with. Sooo much fun running around and knocking them about. Oooh, I feel that tingle again. I think I'll lick my balls; the children won't mind. I'm a dog and I love myself too much.

MUTHA

THINGS THAT HAVE BEEN TOLD TO ME BY
ANIMALS WHO DON'T SPEAK OR COMMUNICATE.

3.

I'm a Duck

24

I want to be a rock star. Instead, I'm a duck.

I want to be skinny and scream-singing in an auditorium of countless people staring and scream-singing with me. Instead, I have a beak.

I'm not even a white duck. I don't have a shiny yellow beak. I don't have fluffy white feathers. I'm not even a mallard. I like those. I don't have one. I'm just a duck . . . the kind of duck that unless you're a duck specialist, you have no idea what kind of duck I am.

What do you know? What I know . . . is that I'm not a rock star. I don't have a band. I don't get to glance across the stage at my lead guitarist as we give each other a look. A supercool look . . . a look that says we have a secret. A rock star secret. God, I wish I were a rock star.

I shit in a lake. Sometimes I shit on the shore but only when there are no people around. Because I find it embarrassing. Nobody likes having a shit on a shoreline. Nobody. I live in my toilet.

I am glad I wasn't born a chicken. For obvious reasons. I've thought about throwing caution to the wind. Trying to beat the odds and become a rock star. You know? Learn an instrument and learn to scream and sing. I tried to get a duck band together but nobody stuck with it. Ducks have no purpose. Well, a duck can dream. Playing pool is cool. I might take up billiards. That would be cool. Have my own stick . . . the kind that splits in half and you carry in a case. "A leather case" cool. Very cool. I think I'll have a paddle around the lake . . .

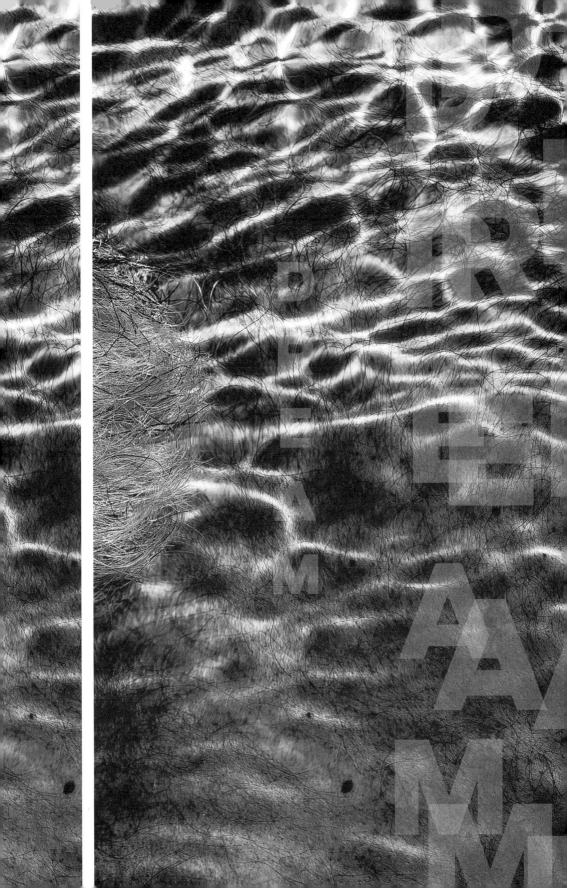

4.
I'm a Frog

26

I'm a frog. Mind your own business.

Don't look at me. I'm a frog. Don't you stare at me. I eat flies. I'm damp. Are you?

You are the one, the ugly one, not me. You are the one who sticks your nose in other people's business. The one who can't keep to yourself. I can. I'm a frog. I keep to myself.

You are the one with the opinions. You have the world in front of you. I have the next stool. My *TOADSTOOL*. You can walk into anything and muck it up. I live in the muck. None of this is my fault; my pond is only so deep.

It is you who causes all the problems; I am a frog.

Stop involving yourself in others' lives. We are not asking for opinions; I have never asked for anything. Catch a frog asking for something.

Never happens. Never ever. I have an opinion of my own. My opinion is not based on anything but a real urge, an urge that comes from my nervous system. You are just nervous. The water is warm. The muck is cool. The bushes are full of insects. Kids like to kill me. Chlorine kills us. People used to have us as pets, now they have tarantulas. Stupid spiders. Large lizards. Sure, now that you can have them, go ahead, get a bunch. Fucking lizards.

My thirst is quenched.

I am not thirsty. I live in water. My needs are few. My opinions, these opinions count.

They are real things. Basic urges. Like eating and croaking. I'm a frog.

You want to be a fly on the wall. Fine, that's just fine. Consider yourself frog food. I'm a frog. Mind your own business folks. You are causing your own problems.

Get it together before you croak!

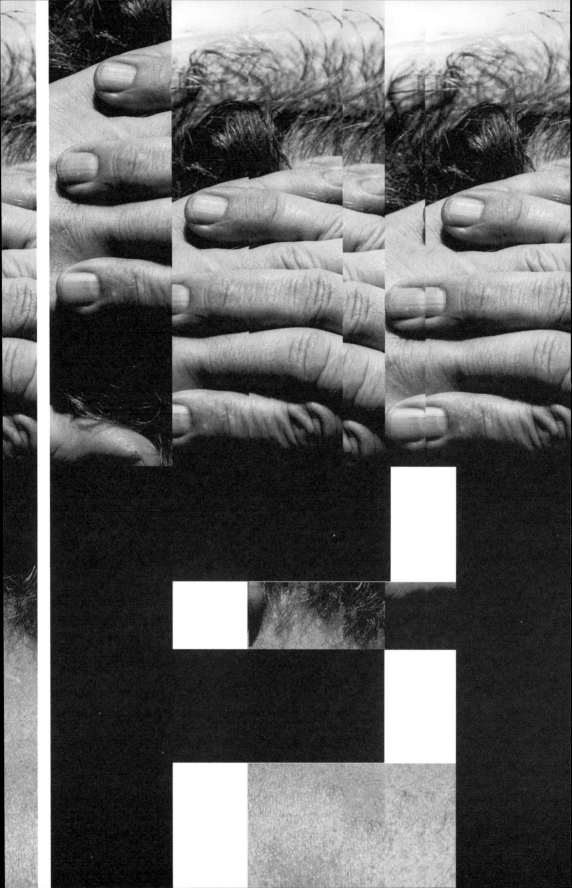

5.

I'm a Monkey with an Organ-Grinding Friend

30

I'm a monkey with an organ-grinding friend.
I don't really like my friend. He does give me
nuts. Hard on the teeth. What's so entertaining
about the two of us? Is this world starved for
entertainment? Are we that far gone? That even
with the Internet, we still need organ-grinders
with monkeys? I'd like some new clothes; this
French sailor outfit isn't cutting it anymore.
If I could get out of this collar, I'd split. I'd run.
I hate organ music; it sounds broken.

The organ-grinder cranks out these tunes.
I'll commit monkey suicide one day. He'll be
cranking out tunes, and he'll notice he's been
dragging me, the dead monkey, for blocks. My
grinder, he's so into himself. He only talks to
me when there are people around. He smiles
at me but never looks me in the eye. Never says
anything meaningful to me. So narcissistic. So
selfish. He believes that his music is worth a few
euros. A few cents, a few. It's not worth a dime.
Not a pound or a shilling.

I'm starting to sound like a *Mary Poppins* song,
but I don't mean to. I just mean to tell you if
I had the chance, I'd take off. I'd open a café
somewhere. I'd pretend to be a small mute
person who doesn't shave. I'd pretend. That's
easy. I've been being dragged around on a
leash my whole life. LET MY PEOPLE GO!
Dragged around looking pleasant, eating nuts.
I used to have a Spanish conquistador outfit.
That was truly uncomfortable. One more thing.
I don't like bananas. I'll eat them because I'm
starving. Always starving. Always dressed in
clothes I hate. I'll bite your ass. Take this collar
off. I'll grab your hair and bite you.

Imagine a tiny French sailor brutally attacking
you. Blame the grinder, blame my organ-
grinder friend. Blame him for the news that
night. When it happens, when I escape. When
I pillage and destroy anything and everything.
The headline: SMALL FRENCH SAILOR FREAKS OUT
IN PUBLIC. Many people injured. A confused
organ-grinder's monkey is missing. A trail of
peanut shells leading to the Thames. How about
a latte? I'm a monkey with an organ-grinding
friend. Au revoir.

6.
I'm a Mule

32

I'm a mule and everybody should just slow
the fuck down. This is what I don't get.
Name two creatures who are known for being
slow and or hard to get moving along. Let's see
. . . um, a turtle and . . . hmmm, me, a mule.
A turtle has a shell so if it doesn't want to deal,
it just pulls its legs and head in and it's off
to antisocial heaven. Okay, now this is what
I don't get. Why is it that while there's this
fucking universal knowledge that mules like
to start in their own time and that we are not
big runners, why is it we are being forced to do
the two things we don't want to do? Everyone,
since the first mule was put on earth, has known
these facts about mules but pretends that these
two little quirks of ours don't exist. Everyone
else has quirks that people accept. What are
we, second-class citizens? I wish horses never
existed. Just a little prodding will do it. Let
me pull the mule really hard, that will get him
going. You don't see anybody trying to get fish
to fly. Let me prod the fish. Pull the fish like a
kite, that will get it airborne. I'm done. I'd run
away but I wouldn't want anyone to get the
wrong idea. I'm a mule and everybody should
just slow the fuck down.

7.
I'm a Cat

I'm a cat in an electric chair. I'm not thinking
about death. The look on my face is aloof. Now
that I'm strapped to a chair, you can stroke me,
even if I don't want to be stroked. Happy? My
last meal is sardines served by a rat dressed in
a catnip skirt. The rat's name is Scratch and
Eat. Fuck 'em. My mind is on strange or high
places that are only easily negotiated by the
feline persuasion. Like shower doors, tops of
the backs of EZ Chairs, kitchen cabinets and
shelves, thin tree branches, and anywhere just
slightly out of the reach of an imbecile dog. Just
far enough to drive the dog mad. Go ahead,
pull the switch. Fry my ass. I hiss in the face
of adversity. A ball of yarn is more exciting
than anything you all can offer. See you eight
more times, you bunch of losers. I'm a cat in an
electric chair.

THINGS THAT HAVE BEEN TOLD TO ME BY
ANIMALS WHO DON'T SPEAK OR COMMUNICATE.

8.
I'm a Guppy

I'm a guppy with a smoking problem. I swim
and swim and swim. There's nothing else going
on in my pond, in my life. My anatomy is less
complicated than a child's wind-up toy. I'm
hardly a fish. I want to smoke cigarettes. It would
help me pass the time, and I'd look really cool.
I realize it's not conducive to my environment,
but I'd really love a smoke right now. I find
cigarette butts everywhere all the time. I'd
never run out, and I'd never have to pay for
them. I'd be a monster smoker . . . two, maybe
three packs a day. I'm a guppy with a smoking
problem. God, I wish I could have a smoke.

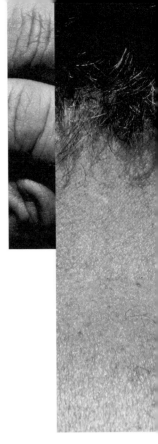

9.
I'm a Hamster

36   I'm a hamster with a chip on my shoulder.
I don't like metal. It's the wrong color. I like
browns and off-whites. Let's not talk about the
wheel. Why should I have to suck from a bottle?
I have a tongue; I can sip. Let's not talk about
the wheel. If you were to take a snapshot of
me, a hamster, and put that snapshot against
different backgrounds—let's say a hillside
or a nice desert scenario or a sandy, rocky
landscape—then put that snapshot against a
bunch of thin metal rods, hinges, and a glass
bottle (let's not talk about the wheel), which
scenario would it seem like a cute little hamster
like me would fit best in? I fuckin' wonder.
And the wheel, this wheel, this metal wheel.
Round and round and round and round. I'm
a hamster, not a trapeze artist. I'm not a circus
act; I'm a hamster. Am I in a way related to the
wheel? I have nothing in common with wheels.
Sure, I run on it sometimes, but if I don't, some
jerk with a smelly hand will put me on it and try
and spin the wheel. Try and teach me how to
spin on it for the one-hundredth fucking time.
I'm a hamster with a chip on my shoulder.

37

10.
I'm a Little Pink Pig

38 I'm a little pink pig and I think I used to be
Freddie Mercury. I know this sounds typical and
that what I'm about to say is an obvious thought
or that it may at first mean nothing to you. I
also know how much it means to me and that it
speaks to me, the real me or the me before this
me, the non-pig me. It's this . . . I really want
a pair of white short, short pants. I've pictured
myself in them with no shirt. With high-top
sneakers and white socks and it feels right; I
mean, it feels like the truth screaming out. It
makes me want to do a duet with Bowie. I've
always enjoyed singing and picture millions of
people watching me; even when I was a piglet, I
sang. When I try and sing now it's not the same
as it was when I was Freddie Mercury. I just
sort of squeal now. It's a kind of squealing that
goes on, a kind of squealing and snorting that
happens. It's not really musical at all but it's
Freddie Mercury-like. Freddie Mercury-ish,
my pig friends say.

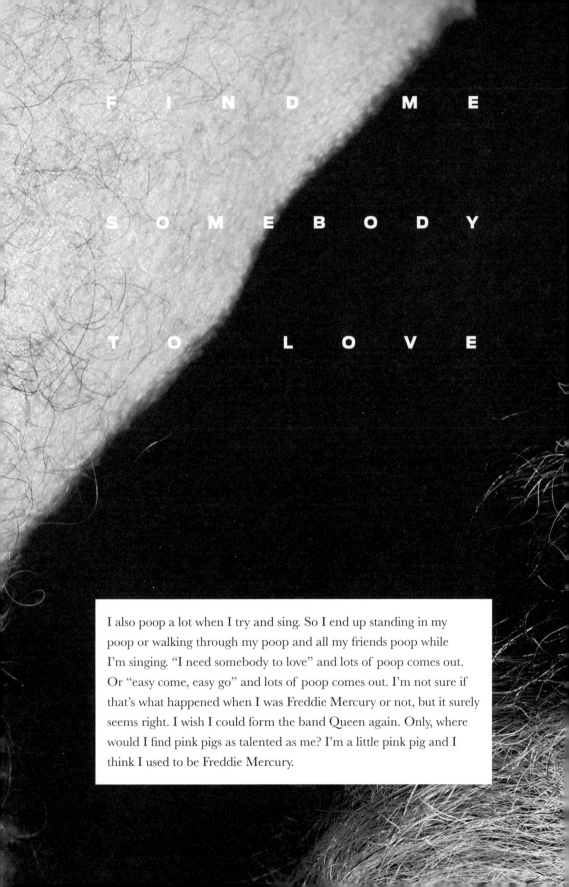

FIND ME

SOMEBODY

TO LOVE

I also poop a lot when I try and sing. So I end up standing in my poop or walking through my poop and all my friends poop while I'm singing. "I need somebody to love" and lots of poop comes out. Or "easy come, easy go" and lots of poop comes out. I'm not sure if that's what happened when I was Freddie Mercury or not, but it surely seems right. I wish I could form the band Queen again. Only, where would I find pink pigs as talented as me? I'm a little pink pig and I think I used to be Freddie Mercury.

MUTHA

THINGS THAT HAVE BEEN TOLD TO ME BY
ANIMALS WHO DON'T SPEAK OR COMMUNICATE.

11.
I'm a Panda Bear with No Pockets

40   I'm a panda bear with no pockets. I love nuts
and certain leaves. There are pieces of root
I just adore. Whoops, I've dropped some stuff.
I love sucking juice out of branches or certain
types of bark. I wish I could collect things I like
to eat. Whoops, I've dropped some nuts and
a piece of bark. I like moving from tree to tree,
bush to bush, stream to stream. I love to travel
short distances. Because I get hungry, I don't
travel long distances. Whoops, I've dropped
a branch I was gonna suck on because I'm
thirsty. I'm a panda bear with no pockets.

I SUCK

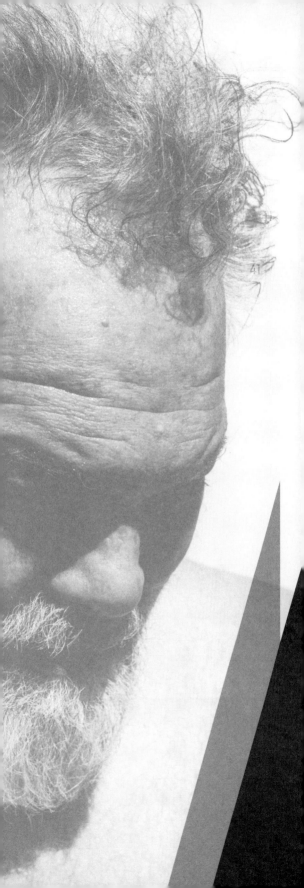

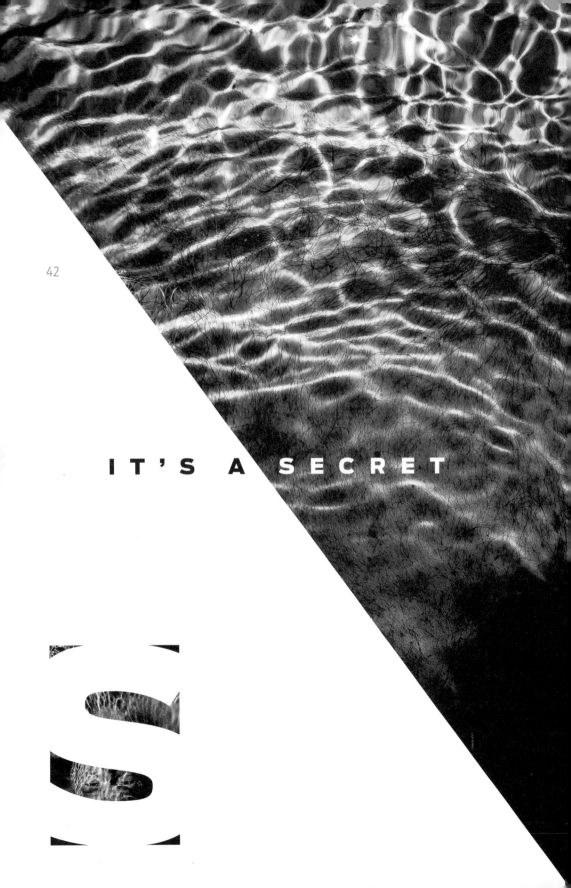

IT'S A SECRET

44

Stories written by something sort of living.
Also me.

2

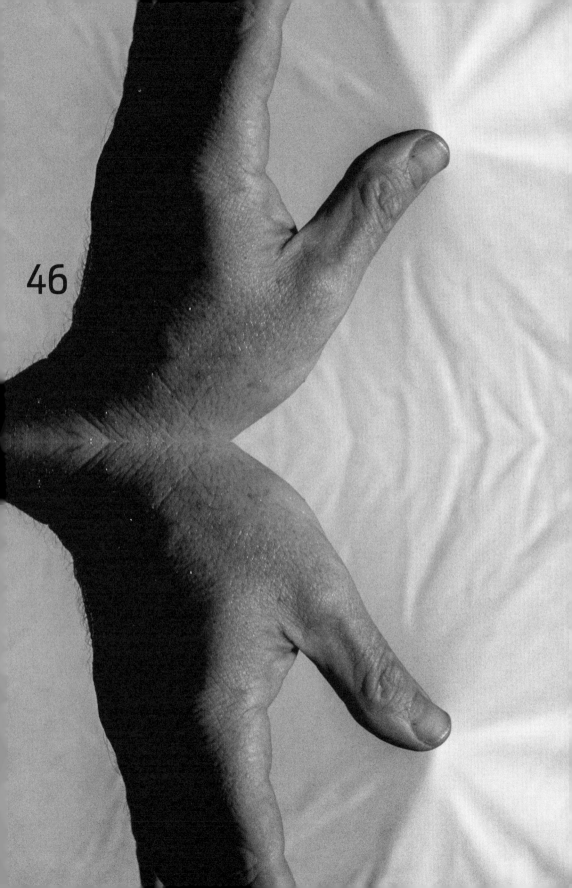
46

48

1.
Pigs Can't Look Up

Pigs can't look up. But I could pick a pig up
one night and raise it into the sky and tilt this
pig ever so gently. I can make sure this pig's
eyes line up with the stars. Imagine seeing the
stars for the first time. I want to be treated that
kindly and see the stars for the first time.

LOOK UP

2.
You Can't Sit Here and Do Nothing

50

You can't sit there and do nothing. You can't sit there and leave your head in your ass.

Men are born wanting to put their hand over a woman's mouth and try to remove her clothes.

Says the man.

Says the childlike adult.

Says the guy so ashamed that it has to be explained to him.

Like a dog.

Don't piss in the house.

As the pee runs down my leg onto the carpet.

Do not shit on the floor while the stench of my poo has overtaken the area in which things are being explained to me. It's disgusting, it's hurtful, you fucking disgusting cock-toting fool. It damages other humans. You've just shit all over humanity.

Do not rape women.

YOU CAN'T

No.

No is No.

Please be a human being and shut the fuck up.

You, priest, who has raped.

You, Judge, who has held down another human physically or who is holding down women by not believing in birth control or pro-choice, you fucking animal. We hiss at you.

Birth control. Really.

Do not shit on the floor in the house. Do not try and rape a woman. Try to be civilized and behave somewhat human. That's what we need to survive. So we don't live in shit, so we don't smell like we are a dying society. A society that can't survive in piss and shit from beings who can't control themselves.

Think of the hurt, think of all the hurt.

Your tails between your legs, crying about and running around, working out. Dopey pigs we can be. Thank you, Judge, for setting us civilized men back thousands of years, you cave-dwelling Yale graduate. And us white privileged old men. Surrounding you, giving you excuses to mansplain your way out of attempted rape.

Shame on us. I don't want my man card anymore.

DO NOTHING

HURT

ALL THE HURT
ALL THE HURT
ALL THE HURT
ALL THE HURT
ALL THE HURT
ALL THE HURT

54   **3.**

Daunted, Daunting, Undaunting, Dauntedness

What is it about this word. *Daunted.* It's
questionable, scary, and lovable—well, likable;
it has a mystery to it even. The feeling that it
can defeat you or a foe even. Just the word on
its own can strike you down. The feeling the
word itself gives me when I say it. "Daunted"
describes the actual definition of it for me.

For lack of a better explanation, it's daunting,
daunted.

I want this word on my side. I want this word in
my armory or on my belt. At the ready.

I want it close by. It helps with the basic feeling of having fear. Or with fear itself. The idea of being defeated by some immense force against me. That SOMETHING is out to get you.

The thing, that thing that's out to destroy me. I want to release the word daunted on it. The dragon was daunted during its attack. I, the hero, daunted that dragon. The dragon was shocked by my undauntedness.

I was pleased by the weakened attack by the daunted dragon. Due to how I released daunting force on it.

The dragon overtaken by dauntedness.

I think I'll keep *daunted* in my vocabulary. I won't discard it like so many other words.

Words I've thrown to the wayside simply because of how they sound or make me feel. No, no, *daunted* will be by my side.

At least until I replace it with *browbeat* or *overawe*.

I'm done.

4.

Gun Hand

I know this is out of the blue.

I've always hated the color blue because of its popularity.

I ran into Pecos Bill the other day.

Looked like his hand had been injured. His right. His gun hand.

The first thing I thought was that I could probably kill him. That he'd have no chance without his gun hand. As you can see, I like the term *gun hand*.

But I like the idea of killing Pecos Bill even y
more . . . or maybe not.

z

But I like the idea of killing Pecos Bill even more . . . or maybe not.

58

Bill then said, "Are you gonna lock up your bike or just stare at me all day."

I locked my bike up to the NO PARKING sign on the curb.

Bill laughed at me. He asked me to not look at him for the rest of the day.

I was about to ask why, in a guilty sort of way. But with a little more volume in his voice he quickly said, "Starting now."

I spent the rest of the day with Pecos Bill. Rest of the day looking down at my feet. My neck hurt. He asked about you. I told him you were fine. "Busy." He said that you should only be referred to as Captain Shepard from now on.

I was going to ask why but then he held up his "Gun Hand" and stared at his hand for a while. Too long really. Then he said, "This hand has been places you wouldn't believe."

I vomited a little in my mouth, and I was trying not to connect the new handle you were given, "Captain Shepard," and Bill's "Gun Hand."

Pecos Bill left me then. He walked away, and as he was walking, I looked at him from head to toe. He was a long stretch of a man.

I wondered . . . is that a limp?

GUN

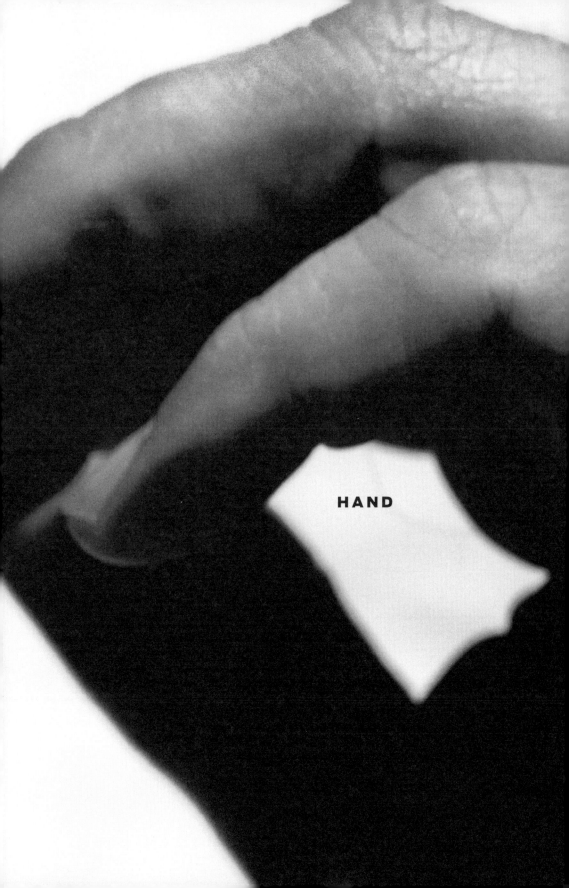

HAND

62

5.
I Blame the Girl Scouts and Their Frickin' Cookies.

I blame the Girl Scouts and their frickin' cookies.

I covet them. The cookies, not the Girl Scouts. After all, they are Scouts and are needed out there.

Scouting. I guess. Scouting.

They have names of cookies I've never heard of, never dreamed of.

It's as if the Girl Scouts have this magical place where all these oddly named cookies are made or created or magically appear. I'm not sure. I am, however, sure of who I am. My name and things and that these cookies are too good. Way too good. So good they shouldn't be allowed.

I should be allowed, I mean, just in general, I should be allowed to exist. I should be allowed.

You should be allowed, but I'm sorry, I can't account for you.

I wouldn't even know how. It sounds difficult; it sounds like a lot of work.

Accounting. Is that what accounting is?

I'm angry with the Girl Scouts. I know they are Scouts and everything, but the cookie thing is insane.

Boxes and boxes and boxes I've eaten.

I told my wife she needs to get rid of them. She bought a whole crate of them.

They must go! I've eaten boxes.

I covet them. All the boxes are wonderful, too wonderful. Too many strange names. Too many great cookies.

So, I covet them.

Girl Scouts must scout for cookies. That's why they have so many.

I mean, if you're a Scout, you must scout.

If I started scouting for cookies, would I find several hundreds or maybe one hundred cookies? A hundred Girl Scout cookies.

6.
I Can't Feel My Head (Version 2)

Today I woke up from a deep sleep. The first thing I noticed is that I can't feel my head. I can't feel it with my hands. I can't feel it resting on my neck. I can't feel it if I turn left or right, up or down. I can't feel my hair or the wind in my hair or the wind on my face. Can't feel it. I can't feel my jaw moving, but sound comes out of my mouth. Not words, just sounds. I can't feel my eyelids open and close, can't feel myself blink.

When everything is dark, I believe my eyes are closed. I think. Yet I can't feel that happening.

Not only do I lack any control of my head, I lack control of anything attached to my head. Unless I'm wearing a hat or sunglasses. Those I can take off and put back on whenever I want. Can't feel them though. I guess that's special. Not special enough to take my mind off of the fact that I can't feel my head. But I guess special outside of that.

It's odd to be able to think inside your head yet not feel your head. It's like when your leg goes numb. You try and walk and your leg becomes this thing attached to you but there's no control of it or physical connection to it. Other than that, you plainly see your leg is attached.

During that period of not being able to feel your numbed leg lurks the dread of the oncoming torture as the feeling in your leg is returning. That godforsaken few minutes. Death by a thousand knives. A thousand knives in one leg.

I can't feel my head, yet I know it's there because I can see out of it, out of my eyes, which are in my eye sockets. Said sockets hold my eyeballs in. My eyeballs, which are attached by tendons and nerves and muscles. I think. Pretty sure.

I'm not exactly sure that's true, other than they are attached to something. My eyeballs.

During this period of not being able to feel my head, it's obvious to me that my eyes are there. That my eyeballs have not fallen out.

I know this because I can still see with them.

I just have no control of what I'm looking at.

Right now, I'm staring at a dog and the dog is staring back.

I could walk away. What I can't do is avert my eyes. The original choice to look at this dog was not in my power.

I'm not sure where the power came from or the choice. Yet it wasn't my head, my neck, or my eyes.

I am inspired to not walk away.

To keep looking at this dog.

Feign some kind of communication with him. Why not? I have no control, so why not exercise my working brain in my head I can't feel.

Does the dog know I can't feel my head? I've never looked into a dog's eyes this long before, and a dog has definitely never looked back into my eyes this long before.

I start to get nervous. What will happen if this continues, what will become of us, this dog and I? What kind of changes, big changes will happen in our lives? How will this long look between this dog and I end?

What influence will it have over the rest of our lives, this dog and I?

I turn and yes, I walk away, I don't look back. I don't want to know if the dog is still looking at me or if the dog has already moved on.

Maybe moved on too quickly, more quickly than I have.

I'm not sure how that will settle with me and I can't bear finding out.

I speed up and realize even though I can't feel my head, I still have the same feelings that I had when I felt my head. The same. These same feelings we all have.

Still have.

Troubles every day, everyday troubles, all peoples' troubles.

Troubles we all have, could have, HAVE.

There are thoughts going on inside my brain.

You see, I know that I have issues.

Regular issues that are personal.

Issues that others might have, do have, HAVE.

And in the end, it doesn't matter if I feel my head or not.

I'm still in the same boat as everyone else. Only in my boat, you can't feel your head. Or my head, I can't feel my head.

Other boats of people lack feeling in all sorts of things.

Could be anything that people in other boats lack feelings in.

Different sorts of dread and such. Or happiness and hunger, to list a few, without me getting too off topic.

70   I'll just wait and see if the ability to feel my
          head comes back.

          Plenty to think about or stare at by no choice
          of mine.

          Uncontrollably stare until that happens.

          Plenty of issues to work through or avoid.

          I'll wait.

          Let's not kid myself.

          I'm still thinking about that dog.

          Did it know I couldn't feel my head? Or not?

          What all did it know?

          Darn that dog.

          Darn my head being numb and the
          embarrassing lack of knowledge when it
          comes to eyeballs.

          Darn the thousand knives of death.

72   **7.**

It's the Year of the Pig, Ladies and Gentlemen

It's the year of the pig, ladies and gentlemen.

I'm a pig and I'm thinking about things. Little
piggy things. When I get very excited I can
poop a little.

Just a little. Piggy poops.

I've been thinking about things. About myself really and who I am and what life has brought me and what I think I deserve and don't deserve. I deserve food. Lots of food. Just pour it in the pen. Any kind. Hmmm, some of that and some of that. Oh yes, and some of that. Oh yes, oh yes, oh my. I just shit myself a little. I don't really need applause; I'm not in the pig business for that. I'm in it for the work. The pig work. I'm all about the work. Folks don't have to say they like me.

I don't mind hearing if they do.

I don't deserve any pig awards. My friends do. They are all pigs and they deserve awards. Lots of awards. There are many pig awards these days and more every year.

I've moved from pen to pen in my life. Leaving my waste behind. My clumps behind me, my . . . oh my, I just shit myself a little. Just a little.

Still, I'm okay just moving forward in pig life. Just meeting that next responsibility. Just paying back what I'm given. Just being the pig I am. The legitimate pig. The pig with a smile. The pig with the darkness when I'm on my own. The pig that doesn't share its true self around other pigs. I'll cry. I'll cry about things later. About all the things I never got and others have. I forget a lot, so I'm hoping I'll forget to cry about those things. Those things that other pigs have and I don't. I might forget it's truly not the first thing on my mind ever. My main responsibility is to be fed.

Like most, I live from feeding to feeding and nothing in between, no extras. Nothing extra for me to think about or not think about. Or forget about, like I haven't now.

I'll take some food if you like.

Any kind. Moist food, dry food. Rotten food. Or whatever no one else wants. I'll even take that. I'll make it legitimate, and as I eat, I'll imagine what a legitimate pig I am. Just mix it all up. Just pour it into my pen. Yes yes yes. Some of that and, yes, some of that, and oh oh, yes, some of that please. Oh my . . . I shit myself a little. Have I told you I poop when I get excited? A little poop, a little of . . . Oh my, I just shit myself again. Boy, is it just coming out. Let me walk across my pen. I'll make sure I spread my shit

everywhere. A little pig shit won't hurt anybody. At least it ain't bull shit. Just a little . . . oh my, I did it again. Oh my, oh my . . . oh my.

In the pig business we move around a lot; we produce, so to speak. Stuff, so to speak. Pig stuff. Shit.

Some folks like it, some don't. Praise is a fickle thing. The truth is nobody tells us pigs the truth. As a pig you learn to not believe a word anyone says to you. Because we are the last to know, because we have to figure it out ourselves.

We overhear people talking sometimes, which is the least painful, whether it's bad news or good news. Doesn't matter to me; both make me feel the same. It's that and/or we realize we are getting fed less than we used to. It comes on slowly. Sure, everything is fine, and then you notice there's no apple in the mix. None. Gone. I say to myself, *Oh, they must have made a mistake* . . . Or, *that's fine, they have no apple at the moment. I'll get some in the future for sure.*

Then I notice there're no used vegetables in the mix and the mix seems to be a little on the light side.

And then one day, you're only getting a half a bucket of corn. And that's when you realize what everyone else has known. Things are not going well. Yet, I'll ask the horse next to me. Sorry, the prize horse. He's touchy. And the prize horse will say everything's good, it's fine, don't worry so much.

Or I'll ask a kid passing by my pen on his way to
applaud the baby goats and encourage them. I'll
say to the boy, "Hey, how am I doing?" And the
kid will oink back to me something vague or an
incomplete sentence. Their pig is just horrible.
They are illiterate. Younger pigs.

People say only a pig can ruin his pig business.
Nobody can do it for them. It's the pig's fault.
And the pig's fault alone. The fault lies with
the pig. Which is a worry if no one tells you the
truth. Not ever. As in, never ever. Oh my . . .
I just shit myself a little.

It's a big day today; it's the beginning of THE
YEAR OF THE PIG.

Now the pressure is on. I can't just be a pig.
I have to represent. I think I'll let the others
represent. I can come across mean or stupid
or somewhat disturbed.

Surprise . . . Oh my, I just shit myself a little.

Life as a pig is hard. As hard as anyone's life.
Pigs just can't complain. We get a lot of grief for
complaining or even having an opinion. People
are like, "Just entertain me, pig, and keep your
mouth shut," and stuff like, "You have no right
to complain while you bask in your own poop
and live the life of the household word PIG,"
they say. And they are sort of right, but that's
another thing to cry about later if I remember
to. If I remember to cry about the one thing I
really am. The one thing no one can take from
me ever, never ever. The one thing that defines

me more than anything else. The fact that I am
a pig . . . This is where my mind takes me on
this day.

As I look at all my shit. As I live with my own
shit and others' shit as well. Shit.

I think to myself and I imagine what the day
will bring. And as I . . . wait!

Is that my name I hear? Or . . . am I mistaken?
Is that my name . . . wait, THAT'S MY NAME.
They are calling me out. Out on the stage. Out
on the stage. Oh my. I just shit myself a little.

I'm being called out. I can hear the
announcement from the MC. What a
large voice he has. What a large, distinct
voice. Perfect for an MC and could be the
reason he got the job. Good on him.

Happy to see folks work'n. There it is. It is my
name. My name, PIG.

I hear him and he says come out, come on,
don't be shy. You, who doesn't want awards
and extra attention. Come on out, you, c'mon.
And I go and I step out and I feel as if I'm
floating across the stage and . . . oh my, I'm
shitting myself a little as I float toward the
center of the stage, and the MC says, "Quiet,
quiet," and the shit flows out. "Folks, quiet
please, quiet," and more shit hitting the stage
floor and then he says, "IT'S THE YEAR OF
THE PIG, LADIES AND GENTLEMEN."

80   **8.**
      A Hard Day's Work

My glass is half full because my mind tells me
so. Drip drip. So so so so much in my mind.
Like a big red bucket of thoughts pour'n over
my head. So much in my mind. I know what's
wrong. Deep down and other times not so
deep. I know what's wrong. We all do. I never
know what's right. Not4sure I don't. I always
know what's wrong. 4sure I do. Much much
in my mind.

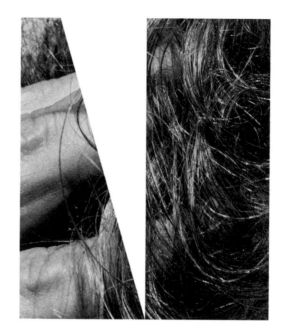

Blast me. BLAST ME. Take me down. Put it/
me down. Take us out. Me, no me. Take me
out. Blast me. Watch the dust settle. Take it in.
Sweep it under the rug. Walk away. Go ahead
blast me, you fool. You foolish gun. Blast me.
Your grave is following you around.

BLAST ME!

I'm nothing. Try it. Reach through me. Look
for me. See. I'm looking at you. I'm nothing.
Nothing more than you. Do you see me? You've
passed right through me. I can't hold water. Not
to you. It's on the floor. Drip drip. I've ghosted
you. Can't you see. Drip drip.

9.
       PATTI

I watch her.

A sphere of electricity, female; she's bounding
around the stage, my vision, my memory—
my vision full of static, like an old color
television with a cheap plastic and sheet metal
antenna, rabbit ears, called rabbit ears . . .
there on stage.

Central Park, unbrushed hair. A banshee, a
seductress, don't let her bite you. Later, much
later. Orchestra, opera house, center, Lincoln
Center. Female soul. Full of soul. A foreign
soul, not my soul, nothing like my soul, sitting
writing. Just there. A visit. A warm visit, not
comprehensive. No telling, no reading, no
hint, just there. Not defined in any way, just
there. I can cope, I can cope, she's human and
needs to sit and be. Surprise. I watch your
stuff on tour; it keeps me happy. I watch them
all. I watch them and they never stop coming.
The greatness. The uniqueness, the power,
originality—it keeps me happy, the soul. The
soul, baby, the soul, it's everything to me. She
continues, this Female, a spout of honesty, not
acceptable, not real, although honest, not real,
although genuinely expressed. Not danceable.
NOT Funny. Definitely not danceable, she
must dance. I know she dances. But while
I'm doing my show I sometimes listen to your
music; it keeps me happy. I listen to them all.
I listen to them and they never stop coming.
The greatness, the uniqueness, the power, the
originality, it keeps me happy, the soul.

84   The soul, baby, the soul, it's everything to me.
I say that to you; you don't say that to me, I
say that to you. It means more if I say it to
you. It means nothing if you say it to me. I'm
done, Patti, I'm done. I won't sit in this chair
anymore. Have it. Have my chair. It's yours;
it's all I have to offer. I give it and she receives
it and I see her there, this sphere of electricity,
this electricity fueled by poetry and tragedy.
A female jester, born to tell stories that lay
in her pockets, written on matchbooks and
napkins and notepaper. Large lint, lint poetry,
stories as available as lint in your pockets. She
searches and searches her black suit; she feels
for lint in her pocket near her breast. She feels
for them near her ass. She finds one. I watch
her; there's static like that old color television;
it's a jumpy image, but I can see her and hear
her as she pulls out the lint and unfolds it and
she reads, "Oh yeah . . . power to the people."

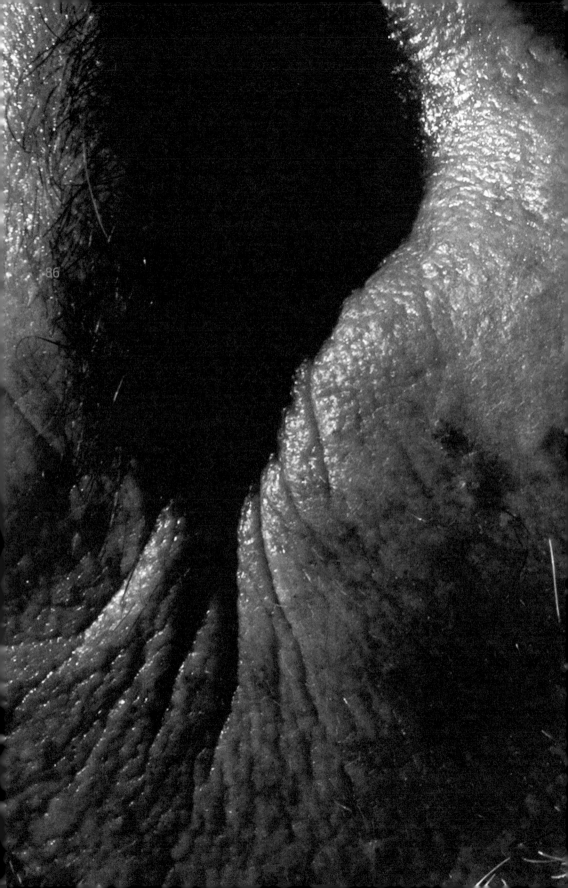

T H E A R E I 'C S
S H T E A T I C

10.
Holy Shit, I'm Fucking Useless

Holy shit, I'm fucking useless.

What will I do about my art? I say to myself.

How can I possibly express myself better?

When will I?

I say to myself.

Will I die not knowing the answer to this question?

Should I pretend as others do that I do not question my authenticity?

I tell myself daily.

How in the hell can I handle my next attempt at one better?

The next piece better,

the next story.

Will I service that story correctly?

Can I help tell

it in a way that is somewhat original?

I will try to contribute to the depth of the story
with my understanding of it first, and my role
in it second, and then third, my commitment to
the execution I have decided to put forward.

Oh yes.

I have.

I do.

I will.

I have done.

And failed.

I have succeeded in others' eyes.

I truly love watching stories unfold.

90   Watching others' attempts to do so.

When done well I can disappear in them.

I let the artist take me.

I want to be taken.

The older I get, the more I enjoy not just the
story being told but my reaction to it.

I take notice of the story and what it makes
me feel.

Still I possess the wonderment of a child.

Oh, I know this.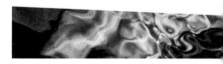

I feel this.

Like you, I know what a child looks like when
caught up in a yarn, a story whisking them
away like a coach and horses.

That can be me.

Is me.

I recognize this as it's happening to me.

It's glorious.

It inspires me to focus more; it leans against my heart.

It causes a push into that ride, to let that wild ride just happen.

Oh my, it does.

Can I always have art in my life and will it be this legitimate?

Can I?

Will I?

I hope so.

I hope all of us can feel these things about themselves.

I hope so for all of us.

Oh, and then these questions about myself can force my eyes closed.

These mysteries about myself as an artist can force me down hard.

92   I see the lie-down coming.

That sinking feeling of that fact, that fact that I
may be way off my mark in life.

That I may, in fact, be lost.

What a mistake I have made.

What a fool I have been.

I was warned about this.

I told myself many times, in fact.

Oh no.

Oh no.

Then, as if it is Christmas, a thought like a
gift comes to me and I see in the far distance
my peers.

The ones I hold dear.

I see them in my mind's eye.

I shout out to them, *hey, wait up*!

I recognize they are my tribe.

I am them.

They are my anchor to this world.

They remind me of my identity.

They remind me that I am not alone.

That they are also in search of the ultimate question.

What in the hell is really going on with . . .

Art.

That notion is my savior.

And then I act out a smile, which reminds me of a smile, which I understand is fake, which inspires me to recognize the absurdity in that.

And then I laugh and that laugh dissipates into a smile.

A real smile . . . and then . . .

What will I do about my art?

I say.

I HAVE SUCCEEDED IN OTHERS' EYES.

'94

I WAS WARNED ABOUT THIS.

11.
I Have a Secret

96   I have a secret:

Do want to hear what my secret is? Does it
matter to you? What if it did matter? What if
my secret mattered?

What if I had a secret and it mattered so much
to you that your life would revolve around
whether you ever found out what my secret is?
It's a secret.

What if my secret was more important than
your life or life itself?

But let's start with just your life first, since
you think it's more important than life itself
(meaning my secret). It's a secret.

Why be so selfish? Why not give into the
fact that it's not all about you? That it's
about everything else in life as well
(meaning my secret).

Why don't you get off your high horse and
experience how the real people live and
wonder what my secret is?

What if we were all just gonna . . . I don't
know? GIVE UP ON YOU? Not care whether
my secret was the most important thing to you?
Not care about you at all (or whether you have
feelings about my secret)?

Selfish, so selfish.

Join the rest of the world. Yeah! Join the real
world where people consider other things in
life. Revolve around my secret for a while.
Revolve around whether you'll ever know what
it is. Make it all about me for a while and quit
being so selfish. Be selfless like me. You don't
know about my selfishness. Keep secrets so no
one knows that you're not really selfless and
that you don't care about anything or anyone.
Go! Go ahead, try it. See if it helps you know
anything more about my secret. Because believe
you me . . . Or me, you. Or whatever people
say when they say that . . . I'm not interested in
what you think.

I've got a secret, and you can revolve your
whole life around that if you want but I don't
care during my selflessness. Go ahead, see if I
really care. See if I secretly don't care. Secretly.

Good luck.

I HAVE A

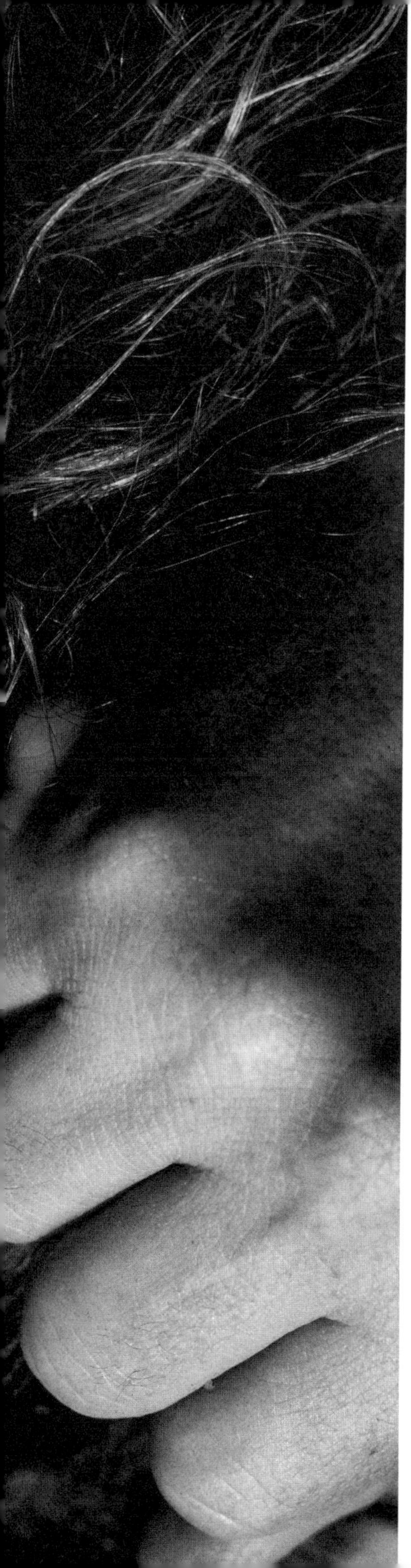

99

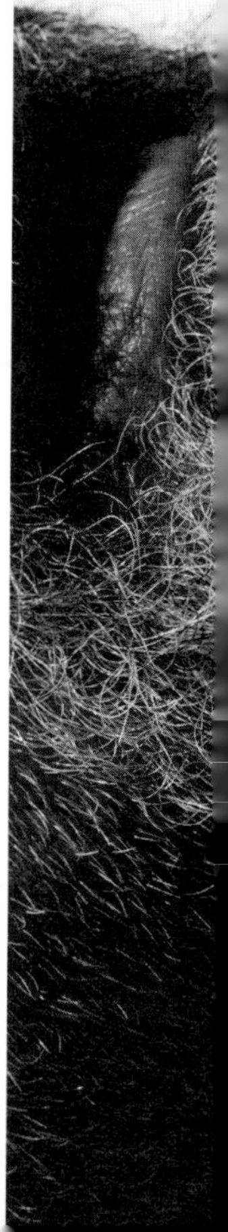

S E C R E T

12.
I'm a Giant

I am awake and I exist; I am a thing, a big
thing. Not a regular-size thing, no, no, but a
giant thing. A giant. I'm not a male; I'm not a
female. My color changes. I can be black. I can
be white. I am sometimes unfamiliar colors.

My sexual preference is never a question.
I feel and fall for others.

I speak all languages all the time. I notice the same things all us giants notice. I take notes. Mental notes. Giant mental notes. I'm not rich; I'm not poor. If I don't have time, I stay hungry. We all stay hungry all the time. Giant things are always hungry. I know a lie when I hear one. It can hurt. I know the truth when I hear it. It can hurt. I can see others' pain. I can reach out. I can feel my own pain. I can reach out.

I can grasp a hand in unity. I can bang a drum to be heard. I can hear others' drums and be drawn to them. You cannot fool me twice and only once with an army. I can be slandered and stomped on. Yet, you must look up to find me. Because I am a giant. I am a human being. I am a giant. I am a citizen. I am a giant. I am an activist. I'm a giant.

We are a herd.

We are a herd of giants and we love.

13.

In Case You Run into Any Woman I Know

In case you run into any woman I know, and she's who I think, I don't
live in New York anymore. Never did. I was last seen walking near the
Williamsburg Bridge with a sad look on my face. Muttering something
about the film *It's a Wonderful Life*, then the muttering trailing off into
something about Jimmy Stewart's performance. Then maybe silence
or maybe just distance. Maybe I was still muttering something, but the
distance between you and the bridge and I grew. All that was left was
what you imagined I could be saying. Comments on long-lost love,
forlorn notions from a lifetime ago. Who knows? What you do know is
that most likely I'll never be seen again. And that I was a good man that
didn't suffer fools. Although I wore my heart on my sleeve, I also played
hearts. I always loved a good card game in the right company. That
you almost said goodbye, but you were distracted by your emotion and
couldn't finish the actual phrase. Then in an angry tone say, "Goodbyes
are for suckers," and rush off.

I'LL

GOODBYES

103

NEVER

ARE FOR

BE SEEN

SUCKERS

AGAIN

104   **14.**

I Can't Imagine What It's Like Not to Be Me

I can't imagine what it's like not to be me. I
hate that. I was leaning against a fence post
and thinking about me and things and stuff
for a long time today, maybe too long. I'm
concerned that others are not aware of what
it's like not to be me. I've tried to be someone
else before. I hid the person I was trying to
be. I hid them in my room, but they made too
much noise. As I was them, I pretended that
some kind of odd coincidence happened when
everyone realized I wasn't. I wasn't because
the *real* them, the *escaped* them, came forward
and foiled my whole plan to be someone else.
Everyone believed they *escaped* them. Not the
them I was trying to be. They didn't believe
an odd coincidence like that could happen.

In fact, they didn't understand what was
coincidental about it. I remember someone
saying it has nothing to do with coincidence.
I remember someone saying it was a little scary.
I wasn't. I think that someone was trying to
scare me or scare themselves. I've seen that
before. But that whole incident seems like a
lifetime ago. *My* lifetime, not someone I'm
trying to be. Not *their* lifetime. I've seen people
try to be me. I hate it. I've caught them in the
act. They do things that *I* want to do. Things
I've thought about doing. I hate them. I've seen
it in their eyes. When people look at me, they
look deep into me, way deep and stuff. Deep,
deep, and stuff. I can't imagine what it's like
not to be me. Always thinking of stuff first,
things and stuff. Things. First. Way first. Way
first with stuff and things. I pity them in a way.
Not in the way that would make me want to
be them and hate them, or focus too much on
being them until I hate myself . . . or hating
them because they remind me of me. Or just
hating me for me. Or just hating me and stuff.
Not in that way. Ever. No. In a more graceful
way, a way that's not so hard on them/me.
Or me being them. Or me being me. Always
kind, always graceful, always me through and
through and stuff and things.

15.
Let Me Just Say Something About Monkeys

Let me just say something about monkeys and their ability to scare the sh*t out of me.

There used to be a monkey-petting place in Florida when I was a child. Monkey World, Monkey Jungle, something like that. It was not a fun place; however, I was taken there many times . . . held hostage by whoever of the other children who wanted to go there, whoever of the adults who thought it was a good idea, and the supposedly fraudulent uniqueness of this place. A place that I thought of as a horrible place, a torture chamber of sorts. It was not the torturing of the monkeys (although looking back now, I'm sure it wasn't the monkeys' first choice when it came to a place to "hang," so to speak). But it was severe torture for me.

The amount of monkey poo everywhere was unbearable. We walked through the poo, on the poo, in the poo for the whole visit. At times, it squirted down upon the visitors. Some people laughed and others cried. All I thought was, *What kind of crazy joint is this? Why am I here?*

The opportunity to feed the monkeys was just insane. Clearly an insane idea. You never really fed them, you just let them grab food from you. Rip it from your hands or body. Steal food from you and run away screaming as if you tried to harm them. Liars basically. Beastly liars, all of them.

I will never forget all the different sizes of them swinging in trees. Hiding in the trees. Sticking their faces out from behind branches and spitting while they yelled at us below, these monkeys.

The group I was with would want to eat lunch there. *Here?* I would say to myself. "Here?" I would say. Among these dirty animals. In this cage where food and monkey sh*t was slung around like cash in a casino. All the monkey faces staring and screaming at us. Faces that resembled something between Teddy Roosevelt and Moe from the Three Stooges. There was an outdoor food area. I was not thirsty. I was not hungry. You would've had to hold me down and force food or drink into me if you wanted me to eat in that disgusting horrible torture chamber of a tourist/monkey trap.

HERE?

HERE.

The screams changed my life. I was to measure
screams and the meaning of those screams
from now on by the high bar those monkeys set
in that place. The sound changed in volume
according to the size of the animal. As I
was being walked out of the establishment,
I remember those different sizes and that
all of them screamed constantly, nonstop.
I remember leaving there and feeling them
over the top of me, around me, everywhere,
and these screams, these screams, from high-
pitched to guttural, loud rolling howls. Feeling
this guttural sound hitting me on my back,
vibrating through my ears and then my face
as I left, and the unbelievable relief I felt from
finally being out of that godforsaken monkey
place. I remember it like it was yesterday.

Later in life, I was working in Rio, Brazil,
a wonderful city. The people are such good
people. Something I will never forget: It was
a very early morning and the sun was just
settling onto the day. My driver was waiting
for me, as he did every workday morning. I
was out of cash so I asked him to wait a few
as I proceeded to the ATM machine that was
on the street. Only a block from my hotel. In
this area shaded by these huge beautiful trees.
As I received my cash from the machine's
slot, I felt a tug on my belt from behind. An
uninvited tug on my body. I swung my right
arm around and felt contact as I followed
through. And as I turned, I saw a two-foot
monkey, with that face. The face of Moe from

the Three Stooges, sliding with a scraping sound down the sidewalk. And screaming, rising up on its hind legs, sticking its stomach out at me and screaming with its mouth wide open. This scream, and the horrid event as a whole, moved me quickly toward my driver and into my vehicle, with the driver laughing at what had just happened and most likely the look on my face and the loss of color in my complexion. The driver laughing a belly laugh as we pulled away, and one block, two blocks, and three behind us now I could still hear this monkey. Screaming and the vision of monkey spit, running in my mind.

Every once in a while, I tell this story when the subject of monkeys comes up. And I always start the story with these words: "Let me just say something about monkeys and their ability to scare the sh*t out of me."

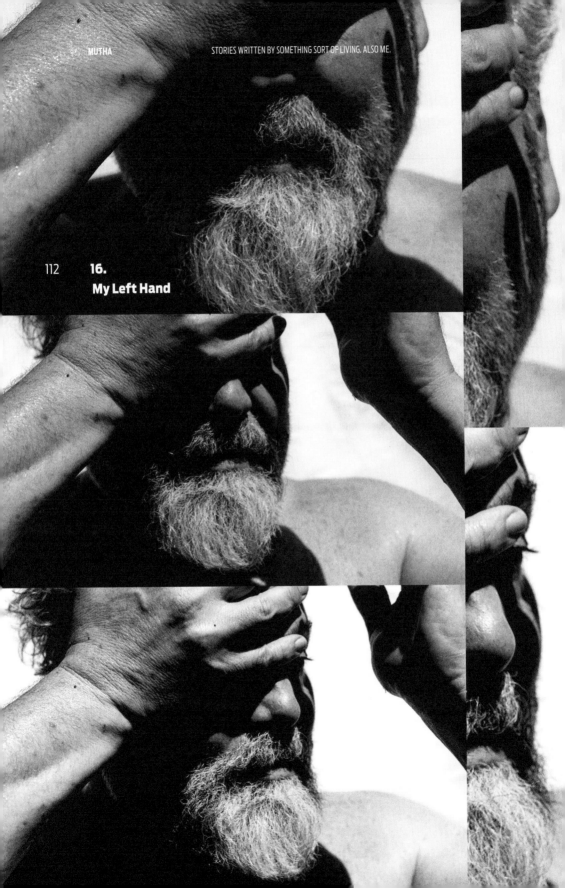

112   **16.**
My Left Hand

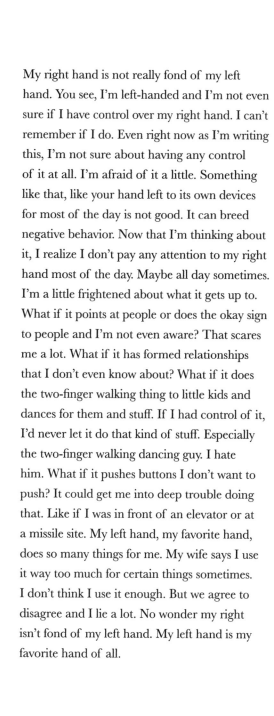

My right hand is not really fond of my left hand. You see, I'm left-handed and I'm not even sure if I have control over my right hand. I can't remember if I do. Even right now as I'm writing this, I'm not sure about having any control of it at all. I'm afraid of it a little. Something like that, like your hand left to its own devices for most of the day is not good. It can breed negative behavior. Now that I'm thinking about it, I realize I don't pay any attention to my right hand most of the day. Maybe all day sometimes. I'm a little frightened about what it gets up to. What if it points at people or does the okay sign to people and I'm not even aware? That scares me a lot. What if it has formed relationships that I don't even know about? What if it does the two-finger walking thing to little kids and dances for them and stuff. If I had control of it, I'd never let it do that kind of stuff. Especially the two-finger walking dancing guy. I hate him. What if it pushes buttons I don't want to push? It could get me into deep trouble doing that. Like if I was in front of an elevator or at a missile site. My left hand, my favorite hand, does so many things for me. My wife says I use it way too much for certain things sometimes. I don't think I use it enough. But we agree to disagree and I lie a lot. No wonder my right isn't fond of my left hand. My left hand is my favorite hand of all.

17.
Pig Tender

My days as a pig tender. Today I was
tending to my pig Mr. Abyss.
I am so lucky to have him in my life
with me, in my room with me, in my
life. I love watching him walk, he's
soooo damn cute. I stared at him today,
stared at him walking for a long time
today, maybe too long. Stared deeply
into him. Truly deep, deeper than
anything. It's not the fact that he is a pig
that makes him cute. I've tried to think
other pigs are cute before and never did.
They just didn't have names. No-named
pigs are clean or cute. Never thought
they were cute even when I tried really
hard. So hard. Mr. Abyss knows me
better. We're close. We like stuff and

things. Sometimes I have to wash the clumps
off him because he could get a rash around his
bottom. So if they don't wash off, I have to pick
at him. I don't mind because I can stare at him
at the same time. For a long time, while I clean
him. Pigs are clean, and Mr. Abyss is especially
clean because I clean him and stare at him.
The rest of life's issues seem to go away. I kind
of fall into him as I gaze at him. Fall into him
or gaze into him, if there's such a thing. I let
myself go and just drift way way down, down
down and away. I'm not scared even when
I'm wet. I'm not scared to fall into Mr. Abyss.
I think I will buy him a friend. I think he needs
a friend. I think I need another pig. Mr. Abyss
would have a new friend, and I would have a
new reason to do stuff. The new pig's name
will be Mr. Gaping Hole. I will probably stare
at Mr. Gaping Hole. He will be really cute and
I will stare into Mr. Gaping Hole and clean his
clumps so he never gets a rash. Pig tending is
really fun and stuff and things.

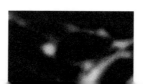

WHO

WILL

BE

THE

LAST

SNOW

FLAKE

?

18.
Who Will Be the Last Snowflake

Who will be the last snowflake.

We are trying to have freedom for all.

Equality for all. The acceptance of all colors
of people, all religions.

If we have to be the last snowflake to cause
the avalanche

that gives the LGBTQ community 100 percent
acceptance in this world,

then let's all try to be that last snowflake.

118

Stories of self while I'm still not completely numb and can still feel my heartbeat and have nothing to do with how I really feel. Ever. NEVER EVER!

3

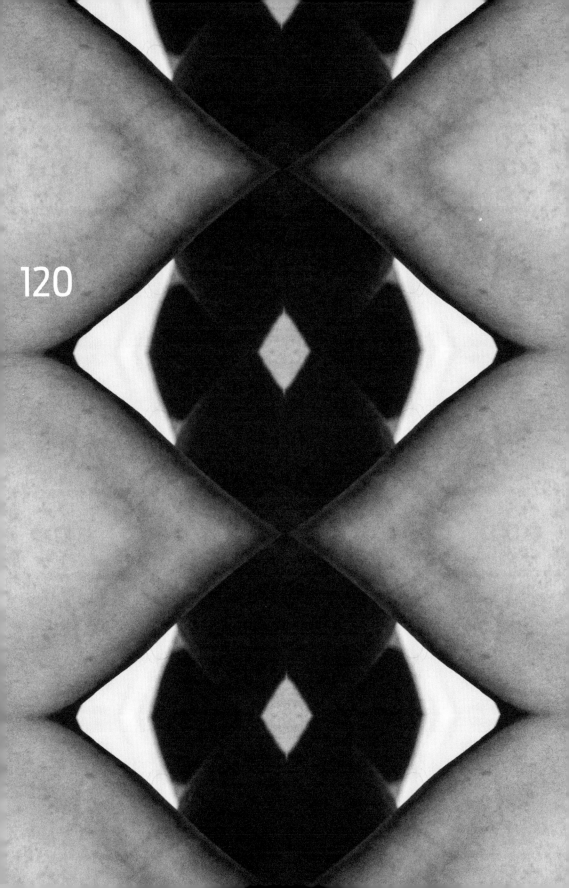

120

1.
Songbird

Journal: I was thinking about how I consider myself a singer. Not just a singer but a great singer. Like a songbird. Someone who sings great. Not just someone; I'm not trying to be coy or mysterious. Not just some one. Meaning some other person. Me. A great singer. I can hit all the high notes. My pitch is perfect. When I'm singing. When I'm in the middle of it, the thick of it. When my voice is sailing above the clouds and even beyond into the stratosphere. I feel untouchable, although I am touchable; we all are, even birds. Songbirds. I've made

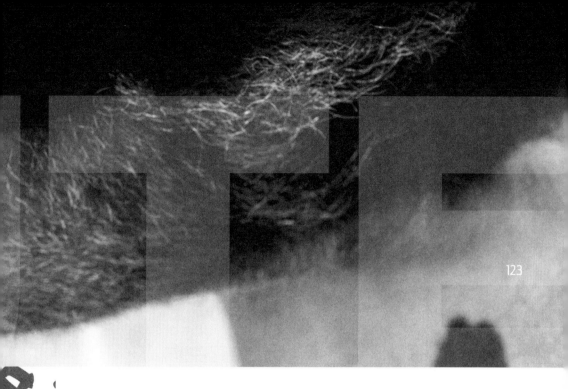

birds voluntarily become mute. They can't handle the pressure. I can't handle the pressure, but the birds don't know that. Nobody knows. Even when I'm in the thick of it, the sadness is overwhelming. I'm crying inside, but what comes out, what I deliver to the world is song. The pain transforms midflight as it comes out; as it hits the air outside my body, it makes a turn, and it's a big turn, a loop, and that loop becomes a wall of sound, a song, and it is no longer pain or sadness. It is something that is left for interpretation.

Interpretation and for muting birds. My singing is great. I'm a great singer. I can hear a bird be silenced. That's hard to do. That's not easy. The silenced birds and me, the great singer. Here I come, hiding and pouring my insides out. Here I come, singing my heart out. Here I come, singing great. I think that's why birds voluntarily become mute; they just can't handle it all. I don't blame them. Ever.

STORIES OF SELF WHILE I'M STILL NOT COMPLETELY NUMB AND CAN STILL FEEL MY HEARTBEAT AND HAVE NOTHING TO DO WITH HOW I REALLY FEEL. EVER. NEVER EVER!

2.
About Thirst and Fluffy Pillows

Journal: This is my second entry today; my first entry wasn't satisfactory. Two is always better in my book, two of everything. I was thinking about my childhood for a long time today, maybe too long. My thoughts mainly involved my infancy. About all the yearning and anguish and thirst . . . about thirst and fluffy pillows. And about the development of my fixation on the number two and round fluffy things or pillows or balls, fried eggs sunny-side up, mountain peaks, soccer balls, basketballs, baseballs, and just round things in pairs. I remember once when I was fourteen tripping and falling into this very, very fat woman's stomach, and when I did, I secretly held on to her with my face pressed against her fat for longer than I should have, maybe too long. I'm not sure, but I could always look it up. There's a record of it downtown. They told me the record was there so no one would ever forget. They were smart because now I could just look it up if I want. Anyone could. I chewed a straw right down to nothing yesterday and my gums were bleeding; I've done that before so that's okay. I hate seeing a litter of puppies and the mommy doggy. I'm not sure why I've written that but I'm sure I hate them. Well, I'm gonna go on with my day and I hope it's a good one, or maybe twice as good as the last. That sounds better. Well, off to my goat-milking lessons; I'm thinking of being a farmer.

126   **3.**

Animals Can't Talk

Journal: I've been thinking a lot about animals lately. Not stuffed animals because all of my stuffed animals got taken away from me when I was a child. I've been watching real animals, not stuffed ones. I've been watching them a lot, maybe too much. I'm glad animals can't talk. I'm glad they can't explain themselves. I'm not a selfish person by any means. Far from it. But

I really don't want to care about anything or
anyone but myself. You know? When I watch
an animal for a long time I pick up on what it's
up to and I refuse to fall for it. Not one bit. Like
when birds hop about. They could just walk.
I've seen birds walking. I've seen a bird walk
recently and made a mental note of it in case
something like this came up. The hopping is
bullshit. I don't like it. Thank God birds can't
talk. Hunters make me angry because they
kill animals, but only sometimes, and then not
other times. If animals could talk, I wonder if
hunters would then kill them all. I can't hunt
because my wife won't allow me to have a gun.
If I had a gun, it would be really fun to live like
in the Old West again. No laws, and going town
to town, and shooting up in the air all the time,
and stuff. If there are rats, why do there have to
be mice, gerbils, hamsters, squirrels, and all the
other nonspeaking small animals. If monkeys
could talk, I might be okay with that because
enough people look like monkeys and enough
monkeys look like people. So I don't think it
would be that big a deal. As long as I didn't
have to care about them. I wish I still had my
collection of stuffed animals from when I was
a child. I loved them. I would talk to them all
the time. Like I said, I'm glad real animals can't
speak at all.

TALK

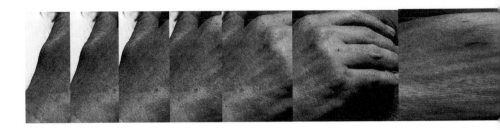

128   **4.**
Animation

Journal: Animation. I want to be an animator.
Or maybe have an animator around for
everyone. Not just everyone, EVERYONE.
Not the kind of animator that makes Bugs
Bunny cartoons. NO. I made the wrong
turn at Albuquerque once and it was a frickin'
disaster. NO.

I want to animate people. Real people, like
me. Like everyone around me. Like me and
everyone around. Not just in a circle but in a
giant circle, a circle that is the circumference of
everything. Everything including everything else
as well. All things and stuff. Around.

I'm tired of hearing myself. So tired. So tired
of hearing myself and hearing everyone else. I
wouldn't care if I was animated. I don't think
I would care. And by then it would be too late.
Too late to care, but not too late to be animated
not to care.

My God, does that sound nice. First in line.
Then everyone else around next. Can you
imagine how wonderful it would be with
all stuff animated. AROUND. Everything
animated. All stuff.

No more whining, no more opinions, no more
ideas. Ideas are overrated. Or they never have
been rated and maybe they should be, to see
if they are up to snuff. No more rules. Or one
rule, ANIMATION. Or feelings, feelings suck.
Suck stuff. I'd rather be animated than feel.
So exhausting, so time-consuming and then
time-consuming and then feelings about that
stuff. That stuff, which has been consuming
all my time. FEELINGS. STUFF. AROUND
EVERYONE. Around. OOOF.

130   No more notions or spontaneous reactions
or actions. Actions don't speak louder than
words, never did. That's stupid. How could
they? You could animate them to do so. You
could animate an action to speak. I've seen
things in films speak that shouldn't but do
because they are animated.

I say animate everything. If no one wants to, I
will. I don't know how to because I don't know
a thing about animation and stuff. Nothing, no
stuff at all.

I won't whine about it, though. I won't have an
opinion about it, though. It's as though I have
no idea. Absent of a spontaneous idea of how
to obtain the knowledge of how to animate.
Nor do I have any feelings about it either way.
No time wasted there.

I guess words speak louder than actions. I
guess we might be better off with an animator.
DON'T LOOK AT ME. Don't even say my
name unless you're animated to do so. And stuff.

132

5.

Ballerina

Journal: I was sitting quietly today for a long time, almost too long, I think. Things got very still around me and then everything just sort of paused. I know that sounds silly, but yes, *paused*, and then . . . a vibration, a sort of surge rushed through my body and pushed me, no, threw me, onto my feet. And then it came out of my mouth like the roar of a lion or how it sounds when somebody yelps when I've stepped on their foot. It just came out.

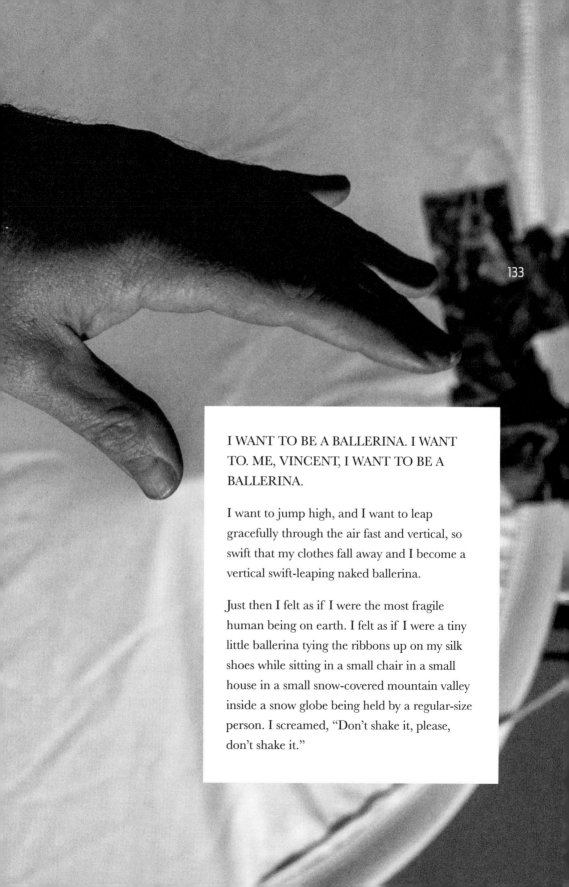

I WANT TO BE A BALLERINA. I WANT
TO. ME, VINCENT, I WANT TO BE A
BALLERINA.

I want to jump high, and I want to leap
gracefully through the air fast and vertical, so
swift that my clothes fall away and I become a
vertical swift-leaping naked ballerina.

Just then I felt as if I were the most fragile
human being on earth. I felt as if I were a tiny
little ballerina tying the ribbons up on my silk
shoes while sitting in a small chair in a small
house in a small snow-covered mountain valley
inside a snow globe being held by a regular-size
person. I screamed, "Don't shake it, please,
don't shake it."

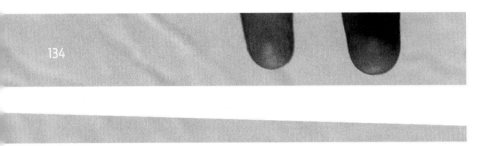

134

6.

Blanche

Journal: No matter how hard I try, my acting career will never be completely fulfilled. I will never play the role I was meant to play, born to play. Conceived to play. I will never experience my true sexuality on stage, my true "real" self on film. Even though, if I may say, everything in my life and career has been leading up to this point, but it will never happen. The public will never see my Blanche DuBois. They will not share my Blanche with me. They won't have her, even though she needs to be had. I need to be had. My past, as hers, was a little loose. My past,

as hers, was a little rough around the edges. The loves of my life are unspoken and spoken all at the same time, in a different time—is now the time? I'm wet with time and time is mine. And she is me as I smell her perfume on me. My emotional life was strong at youth and now lilts gently. Suicidal love, the sacrifice of one's heart and reputation all shot loudly out of a pistol of a young man. When I look at my hands I see I have Blanche's lines. My neck line carries her veins. I'm Blanche, Blanche DuBois. I'm Vincent, the man; I'm Blanche, the woman, the character in *Streetcar*; I'm the character of Blanche in Tennessee's life. I'm Blanche whenever and whoever is performing the play. Fuck it, I'm Ms. DuBois, and I'm gonna go answer the door because there's a young person knocking, and I'm looking fragile, mysterious, and pathetic in a Tennessee way. So don't applaud for me. I hear my own applause in my mind as Blanche and I walk to the door. I'll leave the stage lights on and house lights dimmed and bid you good day, people. I bow and thank you.

WET

WITH

TIME

7.
Conversations

138   Journal: I was thinking today for a long
       time, maybe too long. I was thinking about
       conversations. My conversations. Conversations
       with other people, other things, things and
       people. Why do people talk to animals? I do.
       I do because it makes me feel powerful and
       clever. I will tell my dog who he is and how he
       feels and why he's doing something and what
       he's thinking when he's doing it. Also whether
       it was good or bad for him to do. Sometimes I
       tell my animal the same thing every day, every
       day the same thing. I will tell him at different
       times of the day and sometimes at the same
       time. Tell him what he's thinking and how bad
       it is to think that. I love feeling powerful over
       my animal. An animal like my dog. People.
       Today I felt weak speaking to people because
       I can't treat them like my dog. Can't tell them
       how to feel and what to do to make me happy.

Can't project my miserable life onto them.
Can't feel powerful using them to deny my own
shortcomings. People don't like that. When I try
to do that they tell me to go away. "GO AWAY"
and then I do. I go away feeling weak and stupid
until I run into an animal to lift my spirits. To
make me feel clever and powerful. The thing is,
things don't think. Things are just there, empty
of thought. Thoughtless. Animals think. They
think in silly animal thoughts. Which I never
consciously consider. Nor do I want to.

Ever.

I won't. I can really beat up on things. I can
beat up on them and not get into any trouble.
I can smash a wall. Or kick a chair and watch
it fly, watch it break. No problem, no trouble. I
don't like having conversations with police. Not
police. That's when I feel super weak. Super
stupid. Stupid and weak.

I wonder if police talk to animals or things. If I
was in the police, I wouldn't. I would only speak
to people. I would kick them and watch them fly.

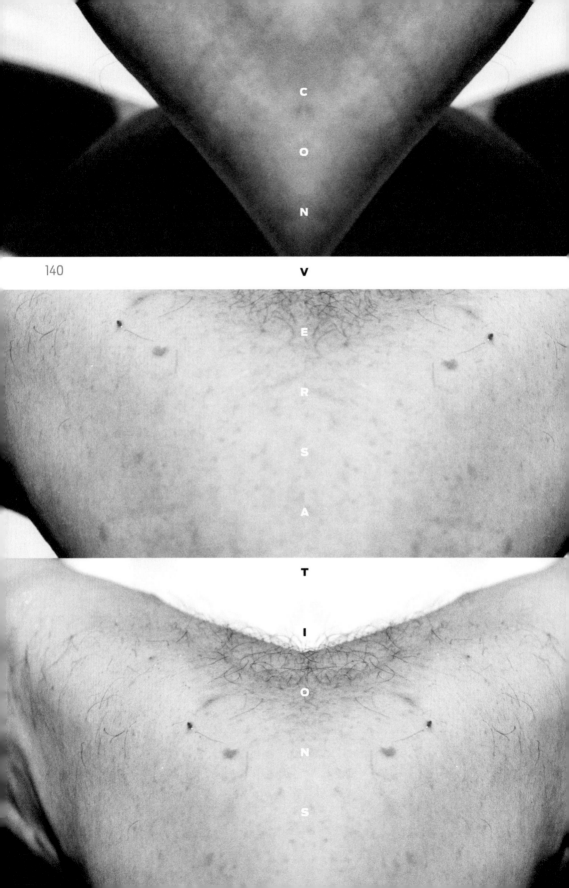

CONVERSATIONS

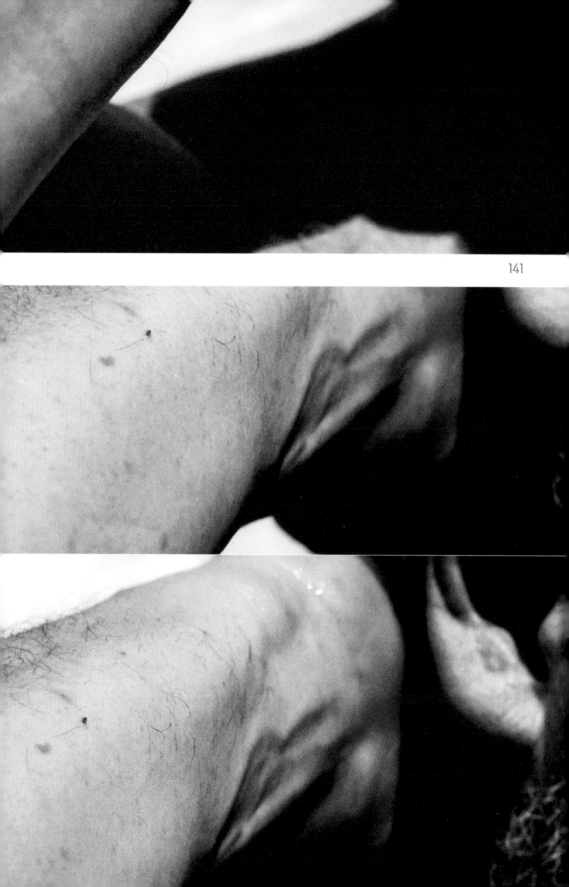

142 **8.**
     Counterculture

COUNTER CULTURE. These words make
me itch.

THING.

What is it? Which right away bothers me. Right
away makes me suspect.

Makes me feel like the wool is being pulled over
my eyes.

Which is weird because that can't happen suddenly. It takes a long time for wool to be pulled over something, especially a thing like a head, because that's where eyes are. On most things, there're eyes. It takes a long time to even say, "You can't pull the wool over my eyes." By that time, you'd know it, and you'd just take the wool out of their hands and chuck it. So that's stupid and you're a stupid jerk. The second you say the word *thing*, it teeters on falling into something disgusting.

144   Do you really want to know what that thing is?

Not that thing, God no. Get that thing away
from me.

And what if the thing is not disgusting?

What am I missing out on?

Give me that thing. Something. Anything.

How do you know about things?

What if you think it's one thing when it's really
another? Get that thing away from me.

I don't want anything around me, nobody's
things. Horrible things. Unless it's a sure
thing, stay away from me. Stay away
everyone, everyone and their things.

See you another time, when all things are
said and done.

MEANDER or MEANDERING.

Please. Give me a fucking break.

Meandering. Please.

I'm so fucking angry; I hate these words sooooo much. They are soooo stupid.

I don't even have the time to say *meander* or *meandering*. NOBODY REALLY DOES. Jesus! Just then, just when I said it, it took forever, and I don't have that kind of time. Time to waste on a word like *meandering*. When I say it, it takes so long I think of other things, like suicide or how to commit suicide and how long it would take and how many other things I would think about while contemplating that suicide.

If you say *meandering* or *meander*, I hate you. More than I hate myself or myself meandering for that matter. Cuz I don't . . . EVER.

146   KISS.

Oh my god, now here's a juicy one . . . kiss.
Kiss is juicy. Kisses are juicy; I love kisses. I
love getting kissed. I love kissing. I don't like
watching people kiss. It's the same feeling as
walking in on someone having a poo. You
weren't invited. Most likely you never will be.

A KISS gets nasty quickly, though. Be careful.
All of you. It's only a kiss. The kiss can be
passionate or sexy, dirty sexy, but then when
you say it, talk about it . . . like now . . . it just
seems stupid. It's something you can do, but if
it's talked about, it's stupid, so let's not talk about
kissing, let's just do it. SHUSH! about the kiss.

MUTHA

STORIES OF SELF WHILE I'M STILL NOT COMPLETELY NUMB AND CAN STILL
FEEL MY HEARTBEAT AND HAVE NOTHING TO DO WITH HOW I REALLY FEEL.
EVER. NEVER EVER!

BLAH BLAH BLAH or YADA YADA YADA.

This makes me itch. This makes me scratch
until I draw blood, crazy blood. Enough blood
to write this. Crazy enough to explain that these
are not words. That they are not funny. Even at
the birth of yada yada yada on TV. TV, no less.
I have an idea, let's repeat something over and
over that was made funny on TV. FUCK ME.
TV. Blah blah blah. THIS is what's funny. Yada
yada yada really . . . really!

The truth is that it's OOSHA OOSHA
OOSHA. Yeah. When you're right at the
moment of wanting to explain that you are
going on and on about the same thing over and
over, you don't say blah blah blah or yada yada
yada; it's much more funny to say oosha oosha
oosha, and it's much more natural. It falls right
out of your mouth like yada yada yada only
much much much much easier.

COUNTER CULTURE.

No matter what other word is attached to
culture, when I hear culture I always think of
me sitting at a diner, and I look down at the
stain left there on the counter a week ago that
nobody's cleaned. That's been festering and
CULTIVATING.

This stain of food, of some kind of old food
now. It's probably growing something, some
kind of yeasty thing on it. Yeasty is gross.
Always. Yeasty things are always gross. If it's
yeasty, it's gross. This growing yeasty thingy
in front of you has, in fact, cultured.

So I find the term *counter culture* difficult to focus
on because my mind goes to other places when
I hear it or see it.

So if I'm not thinking of suicide and other
common things while my mind is meandering,

Oosha oosha oosha

I'm thinking, fuck me. Leave me alone.

I'm part of the COUNTER CULTURE.

KISS OFF!

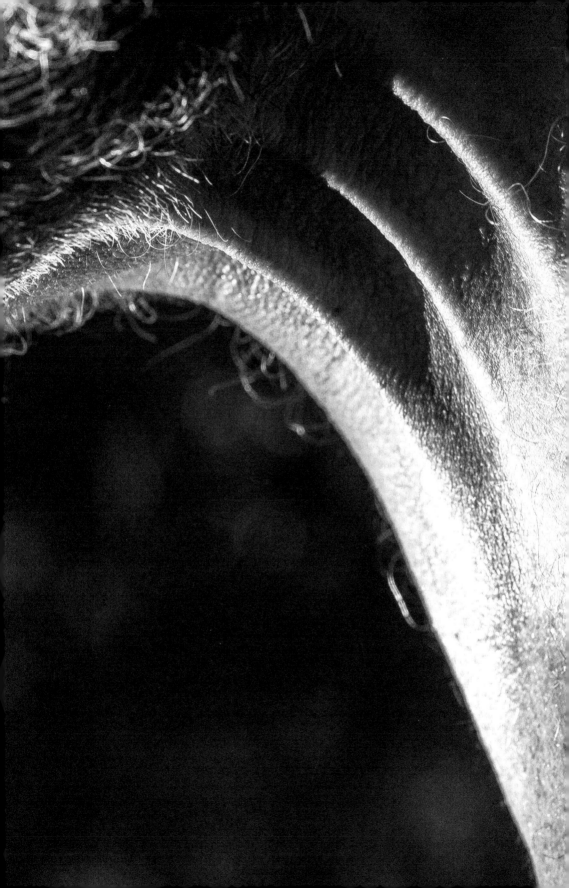

YEASTY THINGS

154

9.
I Am the Wind

Journal: I suck the life from her. Today I realized I am the wind. As powerful as the wind. The most powerful there is. The most powerful wind. If you need a little help down the street, I'm there for you. I am what makes a sailboat sail. Sail along. The beauty of that. Not the boat. The wind. Trees swaying in the park. That's me; I'm doing that. I'm incredible.

I BLOW

When you are chasing your homework down the street. That's me. You're welcome. I'm what makes a dog's tongue flap while hanging out a car window. That stinging feeling on your cheeks, that burning feeling, that's from me pushing the cold hard into your face. I blow. I'm the wind that spreads fire. I jump it from one piece of fuel to the next. Make it leap! Aren't I fantastic? God, I blow.

Thank my mother, Mother Nature. I keep wondering why I haven't realized this about myself before. Why I haven't realized my power? What is it now in my life, now that has made me know who I am, what I am? Gosh, I blow. I really do, I blow hard. I'm the wind. Doesn't that sound right? Doesn't it sound like me? The wind. I'm the wind and I'll let you know it.

Now that I've realized who I am, what I am. How I belong and what I should do with all my time. I can blow this way and that way. I can blow right through you. I have realized that blowing, being the wind is the shit. The shit wind. The shit blowing wind.

The shit.

156

This is where I'm at in life. Like you, I wasn't ever the wind before. I never blew. Now I do.

In fact, people made it a point to tell me how I didn't blow. Yeah. They used to say, "That person over there blows, he or she, but not you, Vincent, you don't blow." Well now, those times are behind me. Those times have been whisked away. Now I've realized I really am the wind and I really do suck and blow. A Windy City. A windy day. Stormy. Brisk and breezy.

I've always been a Northeaster. Today my wife told me I suck the life out of her.

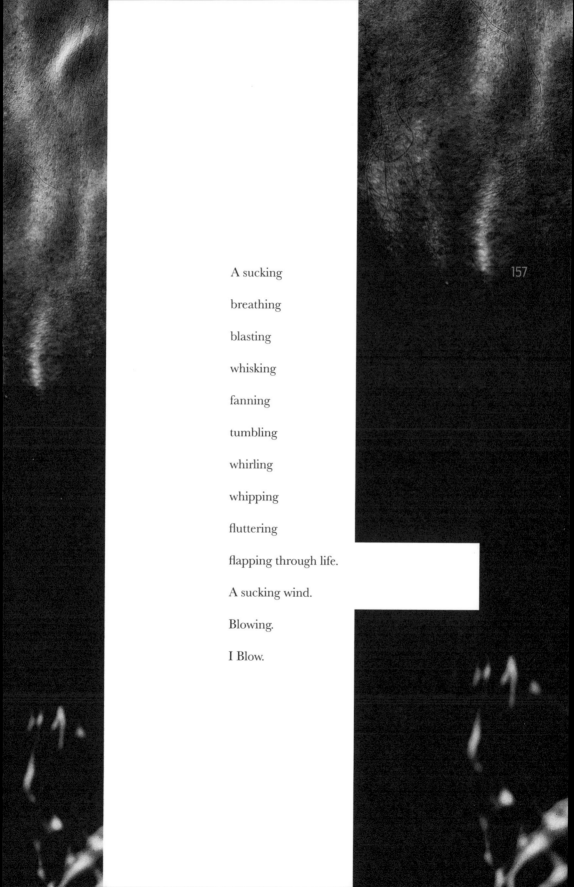

A sucking

breathing

blasting

whisking

fanning

tumbling

whirling

whipping

fluttering

flapping through life.

A sucking wind.

Blowing.

I Blow.

10.
Me with My Western Metaphorical Dustup

Me with my western metaphorical dustup:

How to decipher an asshole? They are a
distinct breed, assholes. Not hard to hear or
see, or for me, to smell even. My nose can
wrinkle from the smell of one of these pricks
or assholes up to one mile away.

I unfortunately have a nose for people who
are assholes, had it my whole life. My problem
is I'm a quick draw, a killer of sorts. A
metaphorical gunslinger from way back.

I'll even take a long shot at an asshole in the
distance. Snipe his ass. Like I said, I can smell
'em. I'll prop my weapon up upon my forearm
and bear down on that asshole; if it's a prick,
I'll aim a touch low. My emotional trigger
finger has gotten me in trouble in my past.

I pull so quickly that folks can't understand
why I come down on that prick or otherwise,
so early, so strong, so fast. I get it. I stay quiet.

They simply don't have the sense of smell I
have for that particular kind of human being,
that particular kind of sludge. My cross to bear.

Even though I'm an innocent, it gets me labeled
in the most darned way. It ends up to be quite
the antithesis of what I was hoping for. I am
then accused of being the asshole, simply
because most folks are unaware of my ability
to smell one up to one mile away.

Gets me the title "Prick," 'cause it don't seem
I'm being civil. Not the hero that saved us a
lot of worthless jibber-jabber and unholy
cracked and smashed thoughts from just
another asshole. Or Prick.

That's all I've got to say about how to decipher
an asshole from just another trusting soul.
I can smell 'em, hear 'em, and see 'em right
before I come down on 'em harshly, and yeah,
too quickly.

MUTHA

STORIES OF SELF WHILE I'M STILL NOT COMPLETELY NUMB AND CAN STILL
FEEL MY HEARTBEAT AND HAVE NOTHING TO DO WITH HOW I REALLY FEEL.
EVER. NEVER EVER!

160   **11.**

I Was Sitting on the Floor of the Shower
Today for a Long Time

Journal: I was sitting on the floor of the shower
today for a long time, maybe too long. I was
sitting on the floor, and I wasn't wearing any
clothes, but I was not taking a shower. I don't
like showers, but I like the shower. I like taking
baths because of the floating aspect of it. I
can float in the bathtub. It's a real good time.
Sometimes when I'm sitting in the shower, my
two dogs peek in to see what I'm doing. Dogs
do that because they're stupid. The stupidity
doesn't allow them to think like people do. You
see, when you take your clothes off and go in
the shower, it's like time traveling. You can stay
in there alone for a long time before another
person disturbs you. Because it makes people
lose track of time. I could also explain it as

being the same as a parallel universe, only I understand it better just because I use the word *time*. You know? Time travel. Unfortunately, eventually I get interrupted. It's usually because the people in my house either need to do you-know-what or it's time for them to get in the shower. I don't ask them what they do, and they surely don't ask me what I do. Ever. Time just sort of stands still for most things that happen in a bathroom. That's where my shower is located. So I try and visit that room and do stuff in it. I can be alone for hours and nobody has any comments about it. Not like they do outside the bathroom. Like in the closets. You know? Also places like the living room, the kitchen, the bedrooms, the backyard, the front yard, the street, the restaurants, grocery stores, bus stops, I can't think of any more places. Maybe when I'm back in the shower I will be able to think of more places people bother me about being alone. You see, dogs are too stupid to understand that kind of complexity. Even when they're thinking about stuff when they lie down on their dog pillows.

That's just stupid.

MUTHA

STORIES OF SELF WHILE I'M STILL NOT COMPLETELY NUMB AND CAN STILL
FEEL MY HEARTBEAT AND HAVE NOTHING TO DO WITH HOW I REALLY FEEL.
EVER. NEVER EVER!

12.

**My Personality Left Last Night
While I Was Sleeping**

My personality left last night while I was
sleeping.

The only way it could've left me without me
knowin'.

Some say it left me years ago. Maybe that's true and I just noticed it was gone while I was having my coffee this morning. Years ago and I'm just too lame to have noticed.

Gone.

MUTHA

STORIES OF SELF WHILE I'M STILL NOT COMPLETELY NUMB AND CAN STILL
FEEL MY HEARTBEAT AND HAVE NOTHING TO DO WITH HOW I REALLY FEEL.
EVER. NEVER EVER!

13.
Manchester,
Part 1

Journal: Went for a long walk today, almost too long, I think. This walk today was one of those pretty good ones, though, because my pretend friend Manchester, my invisible buddy, was not really next to me the whole time. We laughed so hard today, my face didn't really hurt. We went to the steps of the Met and didn't really watch people go by together. It was soooo much fun. He didn't really have hot chocolate with me and kept dropping his hot chocolate. I got burned on my legs pretty bad. But wow, it wasn't really worth it. Wow, it was not really.

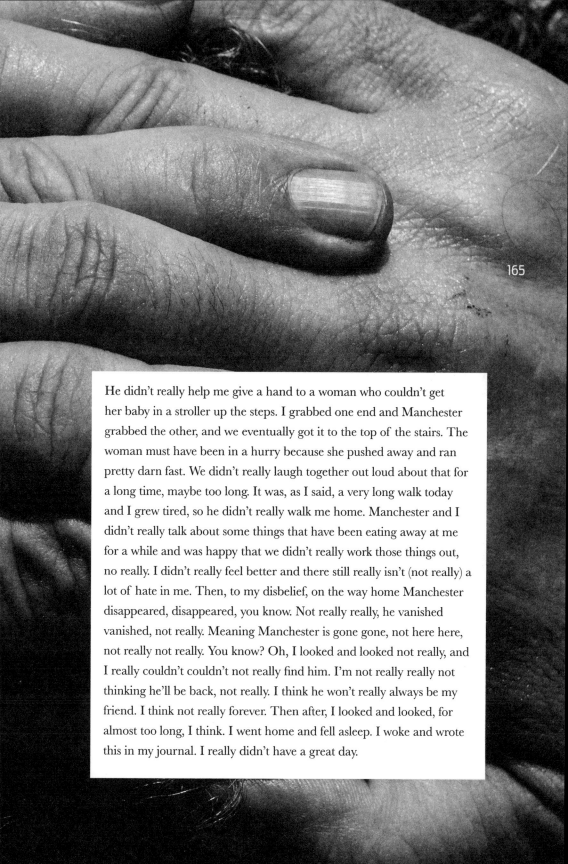

He didn't really help me give a hand to a woman who couldn't get her baby in a stroller up the steps. I grabbed one end and Manchester grabbed the other, and we eventually got it to the top of the stairs. The woman must have been in a hurry because she pushed away and ran pretty darn fast. We didn't really laugh together out loud about that for a long time, maybe too long. It was, as I said, a very long walk today and I grew tired, so he didn't really walk me home. Manchester and I didn't really talk about some things that have been eating away at me for a while and was happy that we didn't really work those things out, no really. I didn't really feel better and there still really isn't (not really) a lot of hate in me. Then, to my disbelief, on the way home Manchester disappeared, disappeared, you know. Not really really, he vanished vanished, not really. Meaning Manchester is gone gone, not here here, not really not really. You know? Oh, I looked and looked not really, and I really couldn't couldn't not really find him. I'm not really really not thinking he'll be back, not really. I think he won't really always be my friend. I think not really forever. Then after, I looked and looked, for almost too long, I think. I went home and fell asleep. I woke and wrote this in my journal. I really didn't have a great day.

MUTHA

STORIES OF SELF WHILE I'M STILL NOT COMPLETELY NUMB AND CAN STILL
FEEL MY HEARTBEAT AND HAVE NOTHING TO DO WITH HOW I REALLY FEEL.
EVER. NEVER EVER!

14.
Manchester, Part 2

166   Journal: Manchester, my imaginary friend, and
I didn't really have lunch today, not really. We
didn't laugh so hard today at people we weren't
really watching together. God, it was fun, not
really. A real thrill, not really. Manchester has
a great sense of humor, not really. Manchester
doesn't really think I'm funnier than him, not
really. So I'm really not really funny. Not really,
really funny. Truly a funny person. Funnier
than most. Sometimes when I'm at my doctor's,
and all the doctors are staring at me, I don't
really watch Manchester laugh. I do that to
pass the time. They ask me lots of stuff. I let
Manchester answer them, not really. I used to
have a new way to talk. I used to answer the
doctors using that new way. But it took a lot of
saliva and saliva throwing and slinging. The
doctors told me it was way too complicated for
them to understand. That never made sense to
me because Manchester and I never really do
it all the time out in the street. I realize if we
run while I'm using my new language, while

I'm using a lot of saliva and I'm throwing and
slinging saliva, I don't get handcuffs put on
me. Which is good because it takes forever for
them to take them off. They never really put
any on Manchester, not at all, really. Sometimes
Manchester sleeps with me. Only on days
that I've specified—Mondays, Tuesdays, and
Fridays. That never changes, that always stays
the same no matter what. Definitely never
on Wednesdays, Thursdays, and Saturday/
Sundays. Like most people, I think of Saturday/
Sunday as one day because I only go to sleep
once and wake up once. That's pill day. When
Manchester sleeps over I like to talk to him
about things like mice, balls of yarn, dominoes,
shoeboxes, masking tape, jax, paper dolls, and
loads and loads of other things. Sometimes after
the lights are out, I do arithmetic in my head
really fast, superfast until I wet the bed. Then
Manchester laughs at me. He tells me how
funny I am. Then I have to go to the bathroom.
That's when things get truly funny.

15.

Pilot Wolf

Journal: I made a huge life decision today. This morning on my way to buy figs, something odd happened when I bent down to pick up some change I had dropped. I felt a little something in my groin. It was a sensation that lasted a long time, maybe too long. Eventually that feeling in my groin went away and I went on with my day. Later, I was standing in front of the arm of my favorite comfy chair. I reached to turn on the reading lamp before I sat down, and that same area of mine rubbed on the arm of the chair—my groin area. And that same sensation filled that area again. Geez, I thought, I really feel like strangling something. I feel like

a wolf running through the forest chasing down
a deer or an even smaller animal maybe. I felt
the bottom half of my body was much, much
stronger than normal. The top half of my
body was completely insignificant. That the
top half of my body was just a mass of flesh
being held there by my pant's belt and other
things, I think, but I really don't know what
attaches it. My brain has stopped working
completely. I have no ability to make a rational
choice or decision at all. I feel like piloting a
rocket if I knew how, blindfolded into oblivion.
Or maybe just piloting a rocket into something,
but I don't know where rockets go once they go.
You know?

I thought for a long time about those feelings
I've been having in that area. If I'm allowed to,
I think I will only stay strong in that area from
now on and not acknowledge the top half of
my body anymore because I'm a pilot now.
My name is Pilot Wolf and my rocket is the
Strangler and I have no top half anymore.

16.
President D'Onofrio

Journal: I want to be president. I don't have to
be the president of our country, although that
would be good. But president of something, of
stuff. I want to be called President D'Onofrio.
I don't want to have to do anything. I want to
do nothing. I want to be asked to do important
stuff. President D'Onofrio, could you do this
stuff? I can say back to the guy who asked me,

I could say no, but then ask them to tell that guy over there to do it. Even if I don't know who the guy is that I'm referring them to. I could just ask them to ask him and he would have to do it. Because I was the president, President D'Onofrio. You see, eventually, he (the guy who was asked), he would ask if he had to do this thing he was asked to do. I would say, "Yes, silly," or something like "silly." No, I would say "silly." I would say, "Listen, mister, that's why I sent them to ask you, silly." He, this guy, would say, "Thank you, President D'Onofrio." I like peanut butter. I like eating it off a tablespoon that I've scooped out of my favorite chunky peanut butter jar. If I were president, I would eat that all the time. Like now. I would eat peanut butter and tell people what to do and call them *silly*. Even if it was hard to do. Meaning even if the peanut butter, the crunchy kind that I like, was making my mouth stick together and feel as if it's full of a really yummy-tasting mud. Even if that's what was happening, I would still call people *silly* and stuff for asking me if they had to do stuff that I asked someone to ask them to do. Being the president, President D'Onofrio, is really hard and you end up explaining a lot about how you've asked people to do things and stuff. Even when your mouth is full of peanut butter.

174

17.
Size Does Matter

Journal: Size does matter. I've been thinking a lot today, maybe too much. I've been thinking about my size and about how very tall I am. I don't always feel tall. In fact, sometimes I feel very small . . . like a small Vincent. Small and gray, like a rat. Sometimes I feel like a rat all day long, scurrying around with dirty little feet and reddish eyes that never seem inviting.

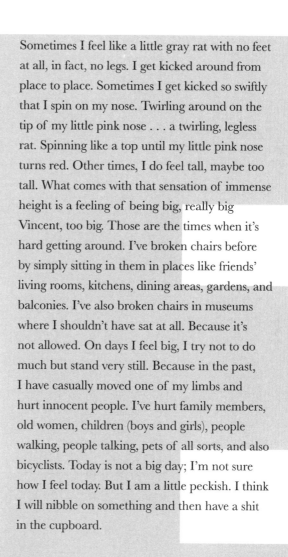

Sometimes I feel like a little gray rat with no feet
at all, in fact, no legs. I get kicked around from
place to place. Sometimes I get kicked so swiftly
that I spin on my nose. Twirling around on the
tip of my little pink nose . . . a twirling, legless
rat. Spinning like a top until my little pink nose
turns red. Other times, I do feel tall, maybe too
tall. What comes with that sensation of immense
height is a feeling of being big, really big
Vincent, too big. Those are the times when it's
hard getting around. I've broken chairs before
by simply sitting in them in places like friends'
living rooms, kitchens, dining areas, gardens, and
balconies. I've also broken chairs in museums
where I shouldn't have sat at all. Because it's
not allowed. On days I feel big, I try not to do
much but stand very still. Because in the past,
I have casually moved one of my limbs and
hurt innocent people. I've hurt family members,
old women, children (boys and girls), people
walking, people talking, pets of all sorts, and also
bicyclists. Today is not a big day; I'm not sure
how I feel today. But I am a little peckish. I think
I will nibble on something and then have a shit
in the cupboard.

DOES MATTER

STORIES OF SELF WHILE I'M STILL NOT COMPLETELY NUMB AND CAN STILL
FEEL MY HEARTBEAT AND HAVE NOTHING TO DO WITH HOW I REALLY FEEL.
EVER. NEVER EVER!

T O D A Y   I S   A   B I G   D A Y

STORIES OF SELF WHILE I'M STILL NOT COMPLETELY NUMB AND CAN STILL
FEEL MY HEARTBEAT AND HAVE NOTHING TO DO WITH HOW I REALLY FEEL.
EVER. NEVER EVER!

178

**18.
Starman**

Journal: I was thinking about my life today. I had bought a pop and
sipped it very slowly with very small sips for a long time, maybe too long.
There was only one thing on my mind and it was truly selfless, maybe
too selfless . . . if that's possible. On my mind was how much I love
being a showman. I truly do. I do it for everyone. I do it because it's
important, and I do it because I think the world wants me to. When
you're a showman you can feel the world ask you to entertain them. It's
not like when people ask you to do normal things like get out of their

way and stuff similar to that. It says, "Hey, Vincent, yeah you, Vincent, starman, showman." I just answer with my head bowed. I answer, "Yes, I'm Vincent, starman, showman for the world. I'm here to give and ask for nothing back; I'm here to entertain the world. Point me in the right direction and don't get in my way or I will get you out of the way real fast and continue in the direction I was going before I had to stop because you were in my way." And then the world sings me a little song of hope, which, in world language, means "please entertain me." Of course, I do so. I will always do so when the world asks. When I'm done, I ask for nothing in return and sing a little song back to the world, which, in Vincent language, is hard to understand because of its complexities and stuff. But it's really meaningful and means a lot. I'm done with my soda now.

MUTHA

STORIES OF SELF WHILE I'M STILL NOT COMPLETELY NUMB AND CAN STILL
FEEL MY HEARTBEAT AND HAVE NOTHING TO DO WITH HOW I REALLY FEEL.
EVER. NEVER EVER!

180

19.
Super Beautiful

Journal: I was sitting and thinking today for a
long time, maybe too long. I was thinking about
how beautiful I am. I was sitting with my legs
crossed, and then crossed again, with my foot
tucked behind my calf on the opposite leg.
That means I'm sophisticated. I really don't
judge people and people don't judge me, on
account of how fair-minded I am, and like
I said, nonjudgmental. People who judge are
not worthy of living, or if they have to live,
they should live in a muddy shack somewhere.
I don't care where. I think I'm super beautiful.
Most people aren't, but I am. The thing about
me, though, is I'm not aware of my beauty,
not at all. When I sit, and I'm unaware of my
beauty, I sit up really straight and lift my chin
up and stare out into the distance. People look

at me. They can't help it. Who am I to judge? Which is a strange expression because whoever made that up has never met me, because I could judge, but I don't. So that person who made up that expression is an idiot. I think I put people at ease when I'm sitting up straight and looking off into the distance. They know I'm unaware of my beauty. I know they know so there're no awful secrets going on. Ever. Because I am so beautiful, I treat my whole body as if it's very very very superthin glass, and if I move too quickly, it could crack and I would fall apart. I try and avoid strong winds as well as overexcited dogs. I try to avoid most things because of my beauty. Things like insects and little children running around. I wonder if they are aware of my very very very superthin glassy self or are they just not bright enough. I won't judge. If someone touches me, touches me anywhere at all, I will break into a million pieces.

Millions of tiny beautiful pieces of useless nonjudgmental glass. That's the saddest thing in the world to think about. I live as beauty in an ugly place. If touched, or if the wind blows too hard, I will shatter and eventually be swept under a rug by some stupid jerk.

20.
Super Golden

Journal: I was thinking about my hair today. How I always imagine having long golden hair. Super-flowing hair, superlong, flowing hair. Super golden. I brush my hair every day for a long time, maybe too long. I brush it over one hundred strokes. They say if you have superlong, flowing hair, you should brush it one hundred strokes a day. I think that's nonsense because my one hundred goes by so quickly. In a flash. So I keep brushing. I collect the pulled hair from the brush and I make big fluffy pillows. I have eleven of them but I never ever show them to anyone. I never look at them. Ever. I only see them once

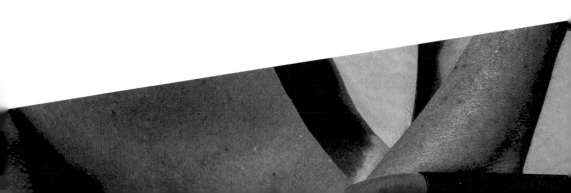

during the stuffing process and then after I stuff them. That's so quick
though that I don't really even see my eleven fluffy pillows then. It's as
if they don't exist. Don't exist at all. Or maybe just hidden. Sometimes
I stand in front of the mirror with all my hair brushed in front of my
face and then, 1, 2, 3, I flick it away, and it's me, Vincent. Vincent with
the super-golden, long, flowing hair. Just after I see it's me, I suddenly
question whether it is me or I question who it is standing there at
all and do I know that person—have I ever met that person? What
happens next is wonderful. My golden hair grabs my attention and
I'm off to brush it some more.

I was brought to the hospital because I had a swollen scalp that was full-
on long abrasions running up and down all the sides of my head. The
doctor asked me how I received the wounds. I wasn't gonna tell him on
account of the eleven fluffy pillows full of my superlong, flowing golden
hair. I didn't fall for that. Sooo obvious, super obvious. Why should I
have to explain what it's like when you imagine you have superlong,
flowing hair? It's hard enough to take care of it let alone explain
yourself and stuff. I'm off to buy a new brush. No one at home knows
where the old one disappeared to.

21.
Tear Catcher

Journal: I was thinking about the way I look today for a long time, maybe too long. I was out and about by the pond in the park. I was thinking about how people perceive me, how people see me. I know that they use their eyeballs to see me, but I thought today I'd take the question a bit further, a bit deeper. I thought I'd just take a while and think about what more is there past the eyeball and eyeball socket and stuff. What do people really see when they look at me with their eyeballs resting in their eye sockets? Do they see the real me? The pretty one; Vincent, the pretty one? Or do they see something not so pretty, something awful and ugly, something so raw and unappealing that they need to turn away and seek refuge? While I was in thought, deep thought, about this, a tear rolled down my face . . . then another tear, and then another, and then more. I took out my tear catcher and caught them all. I love catching my tears; it's loads of fun. I put the cap on my tear catcher and then put it in my pocket. Back where it belongs. Out of the way. The question still looming in my brain, the brain inside my head. You know? What is it people see when they look at the pretty one? I realize that I have no control over what they see, although that makes me angry. I think forcing everyone to see me or to tell me how they see me is possible but could take a lot of time. I would also have to figure out how to get past the eyeballs and the eye sockets. I decided that I really don't have the time to be angry and forceful for that long. I'm happy with the most likely scenario, which coincidentally makes me very happy and less angry. Vincent, the pretty one. After I decided to move on with my thoughts, I bowed to the ducks at the pond and acknowledged how they could see the pretty me. The birds in the trees can see the pretty me, too. I walked home swiftly. I didn't want my tears to evaporate. I collect my tears in the freezer. I collect my little tear cubes. I have hundreds.

188

22.
Tweeter

Journal: I'm on Tweeter now and I'm sooooo cool. Supercool, cooler than most. But that's a secret. A secret is something you don't share. I'm just saying, in case the world forgot. Not that it's possible for worlds to forget. I really only know about our world, not other worlds, so I'll only comment on our world, or better yet, my world. It is possible for the whole world to forget, even if it doesn't happen all at the same time. "Not at the same time" counts. At the same time.

The world is blind. I can see—online. On Tweeter, I make little comments about things I like. I "like" them . . . Like them. I like that, doing the "like" thing. What's not to like? I make comments about things other people like. They can't see me "like." Not me. I make comments. I'm not a follower because I'm a *leader*. I don't *follow*. On Tweeter, I *follow*, cuz I'm soooo cool, supercool, cooler than most. I don't interact . . . interact at all. Sometimes I have to when people are yelling. Or when I'm told to put my hands behind my back.

But that's rare . . . or maybe too often. Not sure. I don't "like" that, but that's okay because I can think about something else and not worry or fixate on times of interaction. You know, the real me, my blind times. When I'm blind and the world can see. On Tweeter, I interact cuz everyone can see, and it's sooooo great, so fulfilling. I "like" that. Unlike me, the *real* me, *unhealthy and not my fault, never my fault* me. I interact on Tweeter. As I said, nobody's blind on Tweeter. We can all see. When tweeting, I'm sooooo smart. Supersmart, smarter than most. Everybody sees. Everyone knows how smart I am even if there's no sign of them knowing. They see my tweets, my interacting, following, and likes. They can't see me, see me. Not me. No, not me. When I'm tweeting, I can't see myself. Not my real self, not me, not the real me. God no, not me! I'm on Tweeter now, and I'm so cool. Supercool, Cooler than most.

But that's a secret, blind people. See you online.

23.
Year of the Horse

Journal: I was thinking for a long time today,
maybe too long. I was thinking like a ninja; I
was compartmentalizing—ninjas do that; they
compartmentalize while hanging upside down,
dressed in black. I was thinking about horses
. . . I was thinking about horses, about how
everybody (and I mean every single body, every
single body, even if that body is next to another

body or with a group of bodies. I'm singling out each body. Even if they are a couple. Couples try to come off as one body, as an everybody, meaning the two of them. I hate that. I only see them as each a single body. I don't care what they want or how they feel, these bodies) thinks of horses as being these beautiful creatures. A horse's eyes so full of emotion, so expressive. Horses do this thing to people, this sort of magical power thing over people, a sort of mind-numbness; horses have a kind of magical mind-numbness over humans. It keeps them from seeing the horses for what they really are. This magic only lets them see them, these horses, as these beautiful majestic creatures. Horses. Nobody wants to think about what's under the tail. Horses have beautiful long manes of hair and beautiful wispy tails; thick, long and wispy hair, if it's possible to be thick and wispy at the same time.

Nobody thinks about how large a horse's penis is, this large and chafed mass that drops nearly to the floor. The horse's lean muscular body, the lines from its chest down its back to its hindquarters, the lines, the aesthetic, like a sleek machine, like the fastest Italian sports car. A horse will crap anywhere; it will lift its tail and poop whenever it has to go. In fact, it's one of the things you can't train in a horse. It will crap; it will poop a small hill wherever and whenever it wants. When running, a horse is mesmerizing; when anybody sees an image of a horse or horses running especially in

slow motion, it's a showstopper, a universal
showstopper. They all, all these bodies, get still
and their faces get all dreamy. Dreamy bodies,
dreamy over horses.

The horse will piss buckets whenever it needs
to. A never-ending stream of piss, which is
fine when the horse is in a field but not so fine
when it's on a stage or if you're standing next

to it. If you're riding a horse and it has to piss,
it will stop and piss, and if there're other riders
around, they will all stop and watch your horse
piss. What if you don't want to be looked at by
bodies on horses, stared at by bodies on horses?
While pissing is happening underneath you,
and God forbid crapping starts happening . . .
If it does, if your horse starts to crap, then these
bodies around you, everybody, all these bodies
on horseback will start making little sounds,
noises, little comments about the size . . . Not
to worry though, no reason to be embarrassed.
None at all, no. It doesn't matter that you're on
an animal while it's pissing and pooping. This
beast that's being watched by these magically
possessed bodies, who are numb . . . These
bodies who only see horses as being majestic
and beautiful . . .

I hate these bodies, everybody, every single
body . . . Again, I'm singling out each and every
single body.

It's a good thing that I'm known as a ninja,
a ninja who doesn't see horses as majestic
creatures. Just the animals, the dirty animals

that they are. I spend a lot of time hanging
upside down dressed in black, hanging tightly
and silently in the dark, my breath regulated,
my breath only used in small increments, only
used when totally necessary, my mind focused
and compartmentalized. Able to think of a
horse penis and bodies staring at me and how I
never suffer fools. My sword bound to my thigh
and waist, my sword at the ready, my ninja
reflexes holding back by a thread, the thread
that can carry the poison to somebodies, some
single body's heart. I shall cut that thread and
spring forward with my sword, spring forward
like a giant cat, a giant Italian-American fifty-
four-year-old actor guy who believes, no . . .
KNOWS he is a NINJA. Should I let my sword,
my ninja sword, catch the moonlight, as I flip
off the rope and my body spins upright, my
ninja silks fluttering from the momentum? And
as the silk settles and flattens, am I a panther
or am I just the last thing seen by this body?
Am I this, this immune to numbness by horses,
who doesn't see them as majestic creatures, who
won't be stared at by bodies while on the beast,
the penis-dragging beast? THE ONE who
doesn't suffer fools. The compartmentalizing
sword-slashing ninja MUTHA FUCKER.

196

Sometimes humanity trips and hurts itself real bad.

4-ish

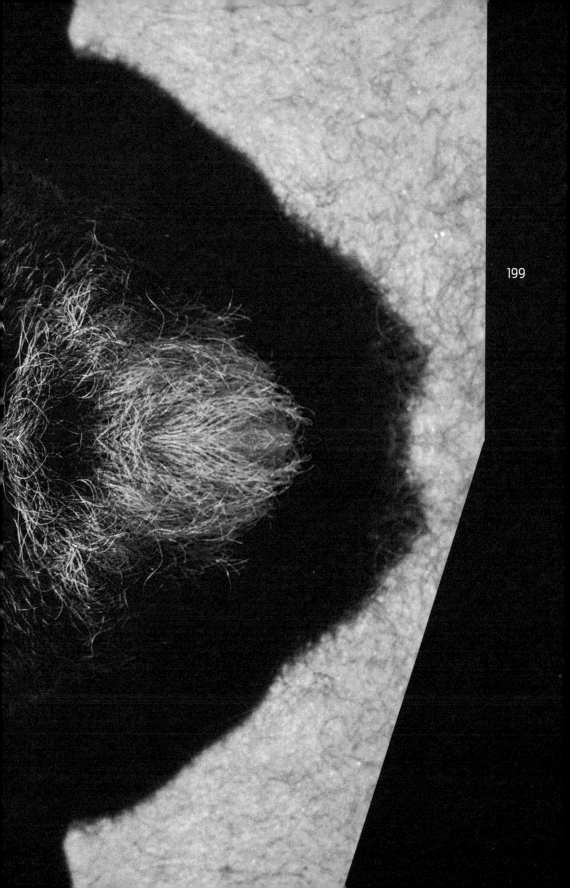

STORIES OF SELF WHILE I'M STILL NOT COMPLETELY NUMB AND CAN STILL FEEL MY HEARTBEAT AND HAVE NOTHING TO DO WITH HOW I REALLY FEEL. EVER. NEVER EVER!

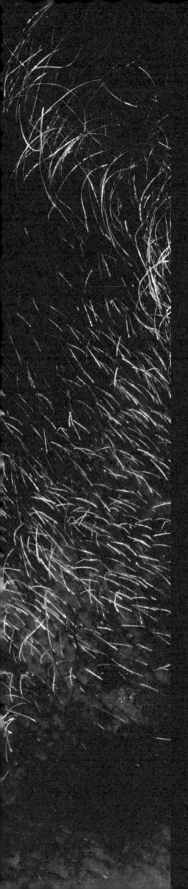

How to Move Through

How to move through.

First,

Always wear shoes in crowds.

Second,

Hold in your mind these words in the shape of
a courageous smile:

It stays with all of us. The awfulness of it all.
It leaves us sad and feeling like we have no
control. We don't. No one does.

Yet we can make choices and those choices
can influence others and those who believe in
goodness somehow find each other.

And that's something.

How to move through.

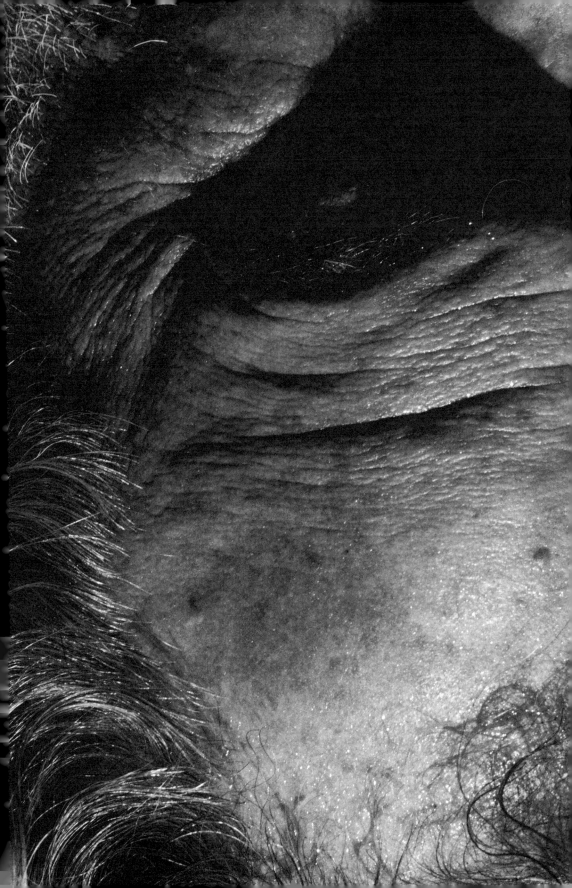

Down to Rise Up

1) Take a knee, take a knee, oh please everyone, take a knee.

One knee down to humble yourself.

One knee down as we look up to goodness.

Take a knee, take a knee, oh please everyone, take a knee.

One knee down for our brothers and sisters.

One knee down to listen, to see . . .

2) Take a knee, take a knee, oh please everyone, take a knee.

A knee down to raise others up.

A knee down to send a message of change.

Take a knee, take a knee, oh please every one of us, just take a knee.

Down to raise up, down to raise up.

We must lower ourselves before we can rise up.

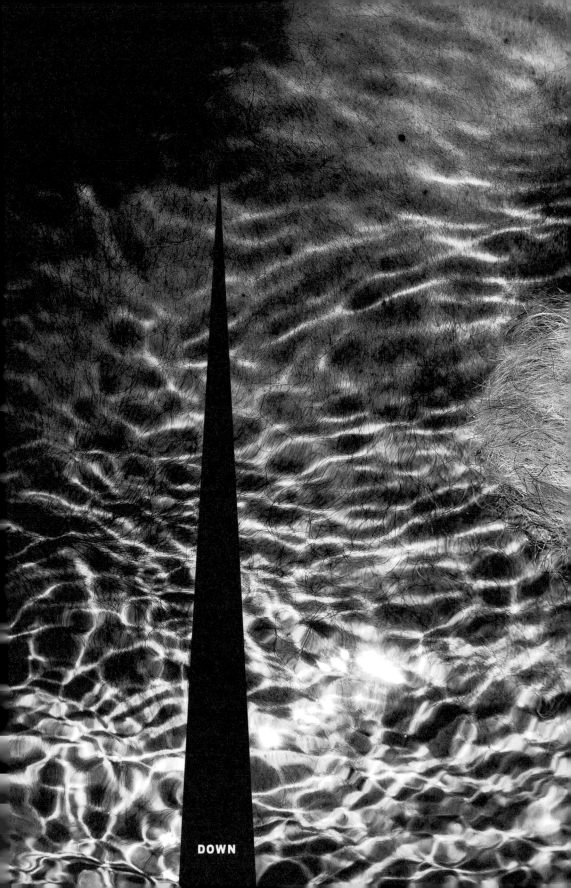

DOWN

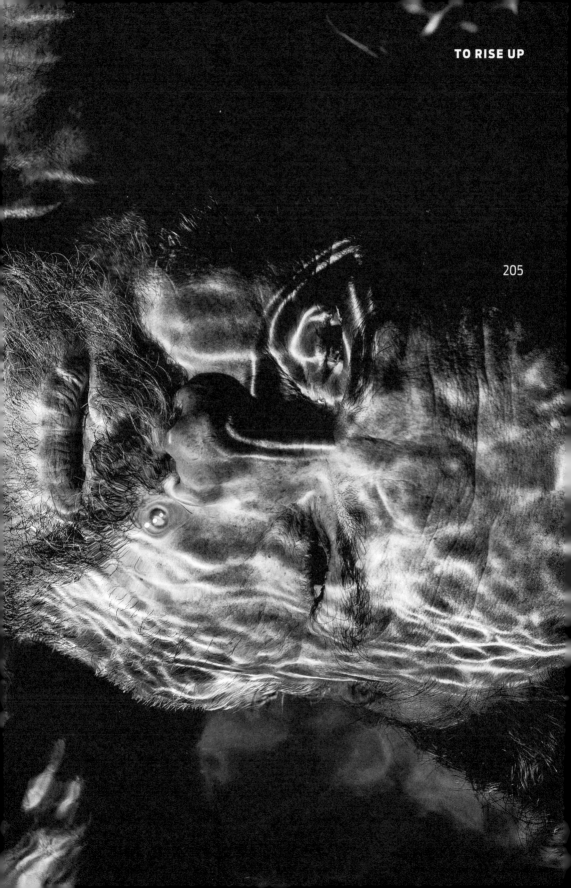

CAMERON + COMPANY
Petaluma, CA 94952
www.cameronbooks.com

PUBLISHER *Chris Gruener*
CREATIVE DIRECTOR *Iain R. Morris*
DESIGNER *Rob Dolgaard*
MANAGING EDITOR *Jan Hughes*
EDITORIAL ASSISTANT *Mason Harper*

LIBRARY OF CONGRESS CATALOGING-IN-PUBLICATION
DATA AVAILABLE.

ISBN: 978-1-951836-13-9

10 9 8 7 6 5 4 3 2 1

PRINTED IN CHINA

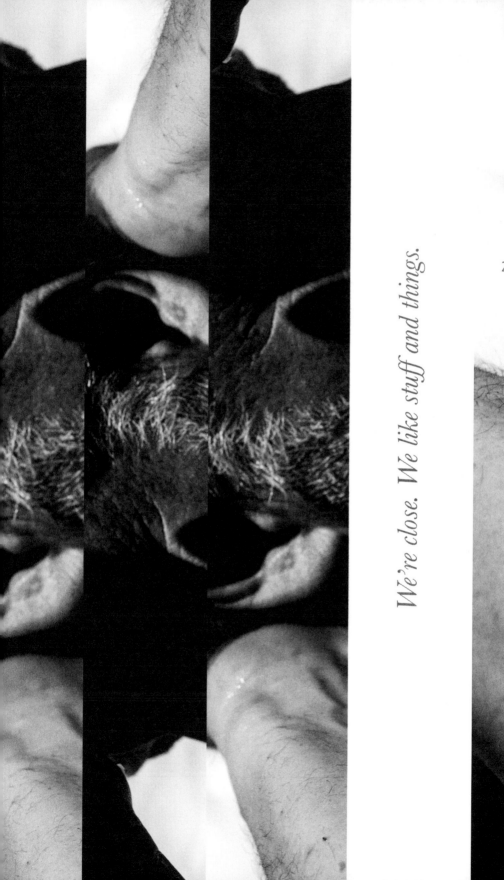

We're close. We like stuff and things.

207

M

U

STUFF
+THINGS

H

A